HUNTED DOWN

AND

OTHER TALES

BY

BRISBANE:
I. F. BOOK & CO., STANLEY PLACE.

MMXVI.

GRAND OPENING OF

THE BRISBANE COFFEE PALACE

WILL NOT TAKE PLACE JUST YET,

J.H. BURNS & CO.,
(LATE C. FLETCHER)

HAVE SECURED THE LEASE OF THE PREMISES NEXT TO GRIMES & PETTY'S,

The Old Grocery Business
WILL BE
CARRIED ON AS USUAL.

OPENED
ON WEDNESDAY 20 JULY

O. WILLIAMS'

AMERICAN OYSTER SALOON (4 DOORS FROM GROSVENOR HOTEL),

GEORGE STREET, BRISBANE.

OYSTERS SUPPLIED

FRESH DAILY

From the celebrated Moreton Bay Fisheries. Fried Fish fresh daily, to be had at any hour with *CLEANLINESS* and *CIVILITY*.

N.B. —Orders from Hotels and Clubs, punctually attended to.

Branch oyster saloon Stanley-Street,
near corner Ernest-Street, off London Charter Bank of Australia,
South Brisbane.

HUNTED DOWN

AND

OTHER TALES.

BY

MARCUS CLARKE.

BRISBANE:
I. F. BOOK & CO., STANLEY PLACE.

MMXVI.

ALBURY-WODONGA:
D&D LETTERPRESS, PRINTERS,
THURGOONA.

TO YOU, DEAR READER,

THIS LITTLE BOOK IS DEDICATED

BY YOUR OBEDIENT SERVANT,

THE AUTHOR.

OPINIONS OF THE PRESS.

We have seen many stupid books, but this is incomparably the worst.—*Times.*

Sparkling with wit and unctuous with humour.—*Standard.*

A book to make an old man young again.—*Telegraph.*

Atheistical and infamous, a disgrace alike to printer, publisher, and writer.—*Brisbane Courier.*

An admirable book for the use of schools.—*Daily News.*

We thank the author of *Hunted Down and Other Tales* for a pure delight which we have not experienced since the days of our boyhood.—*Christian Times.*

The sentiments inculcated by this degraded hound have gained for him the hatred of all honest men, and the detestation of all virtuous women.—*Wesleyan Witness.*

Capital.—*Atheniæum.*

The author conceals a profound knowledge of human nature beneath a mask of indifference and scorn.—*Pall Mall Gazette.*

Written probably by some impertinent schoolboy.—*Globe.*

We have laughed over it for hours.—*Illustrated News.*

Might perhaps be amusing in Hanwell.—*Saturday Review.*

A collection of plagiarised inanities.—*Melbourne Argus.*

We congratulate the writer of *Hunted Down and Other Tales* upon the valuable addition he has made to the literature of his adopted country.—*Age.*

Clever and amusing. He tells us some sad, sad truths.
—*Herald.*

Worth, we should say, about half-a-guinea per column.
—*Australasian.*

It is a matter of wonder to us—first, that nature created a being so conceitedly idiotic as to publish such a farrago of ill-natured lies; second, that any man in this free land of ours is fool enough to read it.—*Leader.*

Left us in tears.—*Evening Star.*

Thackeray without the sarcasm.—*Capricorian.*

Douglas Jerrold without the wit.—*Queenslander.*

The cover seems pretty—we will refer to it more fully on some future occasion.—*Daily Telegraph.*

Imbecile and ridiculous. With this brief remark we dismiss the subject from our consideration for ever.—*Artesian.*

Ungrammatical twaddle.—*Geelong Register.*

There is a levity about this work that displeases us.
—*Queensland Figaro and Punch.*

Should be in every claim.—*Dicker's Mining Record.*

Might be boiled down conveniently.—*Pastoral Times.*

Quitted freely at 2s. 6d.—*Journal of Commerce.*

Breathes a tender purity that enchants while it enthrals us.
—*Australian News.*

Tom Paine might blush for it.—*Church News.*

We have a strong suspicion that the author of this delightful work holds a high position in the Established Church.
—*Bendigo Advertiser.*

Positively indecent. . . . We would put in every honest hand a whip to lash the rascal naked through the world.
—*Climes Gazette.*

Nothing like it since Montaigne.—*Pleasant Creek Advertiser.*

His remarks upon the degraded condition of Victorian society are perfectly true.—*Sydney Morning Herald.*

The author has evidently moved in the highest circles. There is a soupçon of aristocratic ease in his writings that convinces us that he has belonged to the "upper ten."
—*Fremantle Times.*

Might have been written here.—*Invercargill Times.*

We recommend this pleasant little work to our readers.
—*San Francisco News.*

If we came across the skunk, we'd tar and feather him.
—*Arkansas Toothpick.*

Licks old Clement's head off.—*New York Herald.*

The author is evidently an American.—*Bowery Boy.*

Written with taste and skill, but a little patchy in parts.
—*Washington Mercury.*

Could give Walter Scott Waverley, and trot him for a fiver.
—*Picayune.*

Small potatoes.—*Illinois Journal of Freedom.*

The name of the author will live when Milton, Shakespeare, and Ben Jonson are forgotten.—*Nashville Mercury.*

We find it very convenient to wrap up butter in.—*Ohio Patriot.*

&c., &c., &c., &c.

CONTENTS.

HUNTED DOWN.

I AM by profession a penny novelist, and have for some years maintained myself in independence by the exercise of my function.

To some the labour of composition is distasteful, to me it is a delight, and I rejoice when I can escape from the prosaic realities of the world, and tread the passages of my moated-granges, sweep up the staircases of my palaces, hang trembling over the horrible abyss, or grasp by the hands the rightful heirs who have been so long kept out of their property.

When I read that Charles Dickens could call up the people of his fancy at will, and had frequently met and conversed with them in seemingly bodily form, I felt a strange thrill of delight. How blissful must be such a power! Would that I could exercise it!

I was sitting one evening after dinner with the proof-sheets of my latest story before me, when I heard a violent ringing at the door bell. I think I must have been dozing over my own composition for the sharp peal startled me into that condition of irritable wakefulness which follows upon a rudely disturbed slumber. I was about to direct Bridget to deny me to my ultimate visitor, when the door was flung open and he entered.

"What can I do for you, sir?" I asked blandly,

astonished. He was a tall broad-shouldered man in a rough pea-jacket, and scowled portentously.

"Put me into an honest livelihood," he answered. It was such a strange demand that I could only stare. "Don't you understand?" he said, seating himself with rough vehemence, "I want to become a reputable member of society. I want some honest employment."

"But, my good sir, why do you come to me? Your motive is most excellent, but an honest employment is the last thing at *my* disposal."

"That be blowed!" said he, "you could give me a fortune if you liked, you know you could. But I don't want that. No, I'm fly to that game! You'll have some blessed elder brother, that nobody knowed of, coming back from New Zealand and succeeding to the ancestral mansion; or you'll get me pitched out of my gilded chariot at the church door, and marry my wife, that ought to be, to somebody else. I know you. I only want a modest competence, nobody interferes with that."

"Your language is even more mysterious than your appearance, my friend," I said.

"Pshaw!" said he (I never heard a man outside a book said "pshaw"—never), "don't you know me?"

I looked at him steadily, and it seemed that I ought to know him. That hat, that pea-jacket, that knotted scarf around his muscular throat, those brown sinewy hands, those fierce eyes—all were familiar to me. That bundle and that stick—had I not seen them a hundred times in the admirable drawings of Gilbert, Julian Portch, Cousens, Carrington, and Calvert.

"You don't happen to have any marks about you?" I asked, while a cold sweat broke out upon my brow.

He laughed—that bitter laugh which I had described so often.

"I have a peculiar mole on the back of my neck, the tip of my left ear is shot away, my right side still bears the mark of Pompey's claws when he defended his young mistress Alice in the lonely swamp. I have lost the little finger of my right hand, and have three pear-shaped wens, besides the usual allowance of strawberry marks."

There was no mistaking him. It was my Villain! I knew his bloodthirsty nature, and dreaded the tremendous struggle which experience told me was to follow.

"But why come here?" I urged.

"I am sick of it," said my Villain, doggedly. "I ain't to be badgered any more. It ain't a respectable business. First I was Jabez Jamrack, then Black Will the Smuggler, then Curlewis Carleyon, then a Poacher, then a Burglar, then an Unjust Steward, and now I'm an Escaped Convict."

It was true. The unhappy creature before me had figured—in my world-renowned novels—in all those capacities.

"It's getting a little too rough on me," continued my Villain. "I ain't a bad sort—at least, I wasn't when you took me from my peaceful home in the old Kentish valley—and I say I'm getting sick of this line of business. I've a conscience, Mr. Clarke, though you don't give me credit for it, unless it's 'seared' and I'm not going to be plunged into the black abyss of crime no longer. How many pore young maidens haven't I carried off? How many unsuspecting barrow knights haven't I pushed over the towering cliff? How many policemen haven't I knocked on the head? How many custom-house officers—cursing and swearing tremenjious the while—haven't I buried in the foaming billow? How many children haven't I kidnapped? How many wives haven't I married and disposed of afterwards in various ways? My eyes, what a Beauty I've been, haven't I."

It was true. He had done—by my direction—all these things.

"It ain't my pussonal appearance," continued the miserable man, "though what with warts and moles and strawberry marks, that ain't much to boast of. It ain't on account of wounds with axes and bullets and such like that I cares. It ain't because I'm out all nights in all sorts of weathers, mostly thunderous. It ain't because I'm often drunk, always in debt, and totally disreputable. It ain't because I've murdered a large variety of mothers, and brought the grey 'airs of a corresponding number of aged fathers with sorrow to the grave. It ain't because my langwidge is altogether ridiculous, and I leave out more 'h's and put in more oaths in my conversation than any natural man did yet. It ain't that. No!" he cried, waxing wroth, "it's because I'm always left at the end of the third volume, if I'm still alive, without hope of mercy or promise of repentance."

I shuddered.

"Take some brandy," I said, and pushed him the decanter. He took it, and filling half-a-tumbler with neat spirit drained it at a gulp. I knew he would. The Beast—under my direction—invariably took his liquor in that fashion.

"I appeal to you, if that's fair. Is it right? Is it just, guvernor? Your young curate allays gets the gal he's after. Your comic servant winds up with the chambermaid. Your aristocratic villain, the Marquis, my master, who poisons his niece, and shoots his aunt with an air-gun, *he's* all right. He disports himself in the gilt and splendid sallongs of Parry, *he* does. He drives four-in-hand down the Bullyvards, and marries the lovely and accomplished Duchess of Double-Gloucester. If he does get found out, he blows out his brains in the true style of the hold regeem. *He's* never hung in chains, or tuk to Newgate, or starved to death in a deserted drive on the diggings of Bend—i—go."

"What can you do?" I asked, terrified at the vehemence of this strange man.

"Do!"—again that harsh and grating laugh at which so many hapless maidens have trembled; I wished I had made it a little sweeter—"What *can't* I do? Haven't you left me 'anging by my 'ands from a bough, suspended for a whole month over a horful precipice? Haven't I raised trees with my mighty muscles, and bust open doors with kicks of my ponderous boots? I can do anything. But why waste words? Are we not alone here? No sound but the whistling of the wind in the wide chimney of the moated grange; no footsteps but that of the midnight mouser as she creeps stealthily to her prey. Ha, ha! Thou art mine, and—"

Ha, ha, indeed! I guessed how it would happen. My experience as a novel-writer told me as much. Just as the enraged ruffian advanced to seize me, Leonard Fairfield, my pious hero, who had been waiting in the passage of the Priory ever since his return from sea, bounded into the room, and caught my assailant by the throat.

"This, villain, in thy teeth!" he cried (How often had he cried thus?), and pinioned him.

It might be thought that I stayed to lend assistance. Not I! I knew better what was required of me. With a shriek of terror I fled out of the open door, and sped along the lonely road with the speed of a hunted stag.

Black Jack and Meran Hafaz were consulting in the thieves' kitchen when I entered. I knew the cunning nature of the latter, and felt that the thousand pound note I held between my fingers would purchase the secret of the potion. I showed it to him. He laughed satirically.

"That is some of Flatman the Forger's work," he said. "Why did you not kill him in your last chapter ?"

Ass that I was, I had allowed the maimed and

mangled wretch to live! And this was how he repaid me!

Outside came the hurried tramp of feet. They were on my track.

“Save me, Black Jack,” I exclaimed wildly. “Remember when yon were fast locked in Newgate without hope of mercy, I took you out by a subterranean passage never before known to exist, and gave you the hand of the fair Belinda.”

“Ay, but only to recapture me in the next number,” replied Black Jack, with a grin of scorn. “I’ve not forgotten the ducking you gave me at the Lonely Mill. No. Let them tear you limb from limb; I care not.”

My position was evidently desperate, when a new-comer appeared upon the scene.

By his wavy hair, square-toed Wellingtons, massive watch-chain, and handkerchief that hung from the right-hand pocket of his shooting coat. I knew him at once.

He was Sir Aubrey de Briancourt.

“Assist me!” I exclaimed.

The look of scorn he gave me was sufficient to daunt a bolder man, but I knew of a spell by which I could compel him.

“Hist!” I said, in a thrilling whisper. “Proud scion of a lordly house, there is another Sir Aubrey. Refuse me aid, and young Fairfield shall assume your name and title. These minions are beyond my power, but remember you are to be *continued in our next*.”

The threat made pale the cheek even of one whose ancestors had bled on Bosworth, and the baronet waved a white hand towards the back door.

“Take my cabriolet, dog!” he said, with that courtesy which characterises the British aristocrat.

At that instant, the voice of the Villain was heard at the gate.

I need scarcely remark that I leapt into the

cabriolet, and was soon driving with the rapidity of lightning towards Goodman's Gully.

Fast behind came the echo of hoofs. The lightning flashed incessantly, and the man who held the reins was white with fear.

All at once a man clad in a red shirt jumped from behind a bush and seized the head of the mare.

"Who are you?" I cried.

"The most abused of all," said he. "I am the Typical Digger! I am the man whom you and the others of your tribe have made eat banknotes as sandwiches. I have shod my horse with gold and swilled champagne—which I detest—out of stable buckets. Frank Fowler has maligned me, Orion Home has sneered at me, Kingsley has mocked me, Howitt has slandered me, Thatcher has made ballads on me. Do'y think a man is never to change his shirt? Why should I always be compelled to appear in this sanguinary garment? Am I to pass my life in finding repeatedly gigantic nuggets, and being perpetually robbed of the same? Am I to be forever considered such an ass as to give handfuls of gold-dust for a glass of brandy. Must I never shave? Shall the tyranny of the fiction-monger compel me to *sleep* in boots?"

"Calm yourself, my friend," I said, "There is not much harm done. I know of some poor fellows whom the fiction-mongers have treated much more rudely."

At that instant, the demoniac howls of my pursuers were borne upon the blast.

"That may be," roared the Digger of Romance, "but I will be avenged on *thee*. Come!"

The cabriolet disappeared in the distance—there was never a cabriolet yet that did not do so under such circumstances—and my captor led me away.

He paused at the door of the usual bush inn (how well I knew it), and striking three blows upon the door (they invariably struck three loud blows), we were admitted into a long apartment. I beheld with astonishment that all the personages whom I had imagined the creatures of my own too fertile brain were there.

"Wretch!" cried the fair Madeline, "why did you not unite me to the Duke? You know you only changed your mind at the last moment!"

"Monster," said the lovely Violet, "you made me pass three nights of horror in the Red Farm, when one stroke of your pen would have freed me."

"Miserable man," cried Jabez Jamrack, "the blood of the Earl be upon your head. You knew that I had no intention of killing his lordship until the base lack of 'sensation' for your last chapter impelled me to the bloody deed!"

"Dog!" roared Mordecai, "I was born with charitable impulses, and should have lent in peace the humble shilling upon the ragged coat of honest poverty, had not your felon soul plunged me into crime to gratify the tastes of a blood-and-thunder loving public."

"And I," remarked Henry Mortimer, with that cynical smile that I had so often depicted, curling his proud lip, "did I wish to throw my elder brother down a well in order to succeed to his name and heritage? No! I loved him fondly, madly, as you took pains to state in your earlier chapters. I should have loved him still had not Cora wound her spells around my heart. Who brought her to me? Did I of my own accord, I, a proud scion of British aristocracy demean myself to such a love? No minion, 'twas thy brain that contrived the meeting, thy hand that hurled my elder brother into the abyss, and stamped the brand of Cain upon my brow."

"Away with him!" hissed Lady Millicent, the Poisoner. "I knew not of the deadly power of strychnine until he told me. A lovely child, I roamed the gardens of my father's princely mansion, and chased the butterfly from flower to flower. 'Twas he that set the smugglers to seize me, and under his vile tuition I acquired in ten short chapters all the hideous knowledge of the Borgias! Away with him!"

"'Twas he that dishonoured my bills," cried Lord Augustus Plantagenet.

"'Twas he that let me linger in consumption for forty pages folio!" cried Coralie de Belleisle, the planter's daughter.

"'Twas he that blighted my voluptuous contours with an entirely unnecessary railway accident!" wept the lovely Geraldine.

"Away with him!"

"Mercy!" I cried, gazing in terror on their well-known lineaments. "Mercy!"

"Mercy!" cried the Lost Heiress, Isabelle Beaumanoir, "when for two long hours you deliberated whether my sainted mother or the poacher's wife should give me birth! Mercy for *thee*! Oh, no, no, no!"

"Ladies and gentlemen," cried I in despair, "consider the exigencies of fiction!"

"Fiction be blowed!" roared the Digger. "This way, boys." A deserted drive was before me—how many luckless wretches had not I thrown down it?—and I made one supreme effort.

"Ladies and gentlemen," I shouted, "consider dramatic unity! You could not all be happy!"

"Dramatic unity be d——!" snarled Jabez Jamrack, "that is the last thing you thought of!"

I trembled over the abyss.

"Hold!" said the rough voice of my Villain, who had now approached. "Make me respectable, and you shall live!"

"I can't," I said faintly. "It is impossible. You are too great a ruffian."

"Let go!" cried the Digger, and I already felt myself launched into the chasm, when a loud ringing sounded in my ears, and I heard the voice of Leonard Fairfield. The noble fellow had sprung the alarm-bell!

"Fiends!" he shouted with all the force of his lungs—ha! ha! 'twas I that gave them to him!—"Thou aft baffled! Back, Demon! Thy limbs shall feed the ravens, and the magpie perch upon thy fleshless skull! What ho! Without there!"

"Why seek to dispel my *ennui* with this *espieglerie, mon ami*," said the soft tones of the Count in his native tongue. "*Sacré*, let the *pauvre petit* escape, my *déjeuner à la fourchette* awaits. The *coup d'oeil* is superb, the *tout ensemble* all that could be desired. *Voila!*"

The digger swung me over the yawning grave. All the buttons in my waistcoat gave way, and for an instant my life hung literally by a thread.

"Will you make me respectable?" said the Villain.

"Never."

The button cracked. I was going, going—gone, when the alarm-bell sounded, the door was burst open, and

---

Bridget entered.

"It is the boy from the printers' for the proofs," said she.

"Tell him to wait," said I; and wiping the sweat from my intellectual brow, I seized my pen, and in ten lines had got my Villain comfortably in irons at Norfolk Island.

THE POOR ARTIST.

"THERE is a fellow who has been painting some picture," my editor had said, handing me a note written in a woman's handwriting. "I wish you would go down and have a look at it. He wants a notice, or something." *Mr. Bell, artist, the studio, 3005 Bourke-street* was on the printed card, and I called the next day. The studio was difficult to approach, for the building in Bourke-street was one of those overgrown places in which a dozen trades are carried on under one roof. The ground floor (bisected by the staircase) was occupied by a hairdressing tobacconist on the one side, and an umbrella-maker on the other. On the second floor, Messrs. Gripe and Squezem, solicitors and proctors, had established their offices. On the third floor, two working jewellers, an engraver, and a myall-wood pipe-maker burrowed together, and on the top of the fourth flight of stairs lived Mr. Bell. A glass door with the word "studio" on it gave token of his artistic claims, and a sort of aerial conservatory strongly smelling of collodion, and littered with photographic portraits, betrayed his profession.

Getting no reply to a knock at the studio door, I turned into the photographic-room, and, with an unpleasant feeling that someone was inspecting me from the purblind window of the "dark-house," sat upon a chair, and awaited the advent of somebody connected with the establishment. There is to me nothing more depressing to contemplate than the photographs of common-place people; for such folk—worthy citizens in ordinary working days—indulge, on such occasions, in such monstrosities of costume, and in such sadly ludicrous assumption of ease and wealth, that the tender-hearted spectator cannot but sigh at the horrible evidences of the prevalence of "Sham." A "group" (Father, Mother, Mary, Jane, Tommy, Sukey, Jacky, and Baby) which, gorgeously painted, and framed in stamped leather-work to imitate oak, had attracted my attention by reason of the amount of gold leaf expended on the family electro-plate, caused me to wonder what artist could endure life among such vulgarities, when the door opened, and a middle-aged lady entered. She was dressed in greasy black, was busily rubbing her hands as though she had but just washed them, and from certain sucking noises made by the twitching of her lips, I concluded that I had disturbed her at an early dinner. When she saw that I was alone, a certain heartiness of welcome, which had marked her hasty entrance, vanished.

She had expected a "group," perhaps.

"Is this Mr. Bell's studio?" I asked.

"It is, sir."

"I have—um—called to see a picture," producing the letter.

"Oh! Certainly. From the *Peacock* office? Mr. Bell is out just now—my son, sir—but it's in the stoodio. Will you sit down a moment? I didn't expect you so soon. Dear, dear, if Tom had only been at home now!"

Mrs. Bell retired, and from certain whisperings which reached me, mingled with the muffled clattering of plates, I concluded that the studio was sometimes devoted to the study of the art of dining. Presently she reappeared in a clean apron and another cap (women can on occasions make such changes of costume with the rapidity of pantomimists), and smiling, led the way.

The studio was a large, bare room, hung round with casts of feet, clenched hands, and flowers. Some photographs were strewn upon a table. A violin depended from a nail. In one corner was a cupboard. The "dinner" was upon a tray with a cloth thrown over it. At the further end of the room stood an easel of portentous size, and on the easel stood It.

"I am *so* sorry Tom is out," repeated Mrs. Bell. "But he gives lessons, you see, sir, and he's gone to Hawthorn this afternoon. You might wait, sir; but it is a long walk, and he started later than usual today. However, of course, you can judge, you know, sir, just as well; but I *wish* Tom had been here."

I stood before the canvas. A tall man, dressed in flowing robes and crowned with feathers, occupied the centre of the picture, leaning on the arms of two other feather-bearers. Over the heads of the trio, two brown, half-naked slaves held a canopy, which also sprouted with plumes. On the right hand, and in the extreme foreground, stood a man in armour, with a woman dressed in boy's clothes holding the bridle of a horse whose nose only was visible. A priest talked to another man in armour on the left, and in the background arose the ruins of a windmill.

"Pray, madam, what is the subject of this work?"

"It's Cortez, sir. Cortez meeting the King of Mexico after burning the capital." The windmill, then, was a sacrificial tower.

One glance was enough. Had I been alone I should have turned on my heel and departed straightway. The figures were not in drawing, the background was not in perspective, the composition was common-place. But the anxious eyes and restless hands of the poor mother forbade me to quit without the utterance of some cheering platitude.

"Mr. Bell has spent some time over this?" I hazarded.

"Indeed he has, sir—worked at it from daylight till dark (often when he might have been earning money, too); but he's devoted to his art, Tom is. You see, sir, he always had a taste for drawing, and went to a school of design, and that, and worked hard at it. Photography pays best, though, as I tell him, but he will be a painter, sir. He thinks—he hopes—oh, *what* do you think of it, sir?"

"Your son has been very careful."

"He has, sir. The books he's read to get ideas, too! But there, you see—I'll send for Polly, she can talk about it better than I—Polly!"

Polly was evidently Mrs. Tom, and, unless my ears deceived me, I heard the querulous wail of a sickly infant from the adjoining room.

"She is quite an artist, Polly is," said Mrs. Bell, as the dark-eyed, slim girl removed a paint-brush, which she blushingly remembered was sticking behind her ear. "Tom often says he wouldn't know what to do without Polly." It was evident that Polly coloured the photographs.

"I am sorry that Mr. Bell is out," said she; "but—if you will allow me I will move it a little, so—now you get a better light, see. You know the story of Montezuma, sir?"

"I have heard it."

"Mr. Bell has seized the moment when the fallen sovereign approaches leaning on the arms of his brothers. Cortez you see in the foreground with his wife, Marina, holding his horse. The priest on the left is Father Olmedo. Mr. Bell copied it from an engraving."

"The head of the priest, you mean?"

"Yes," she returned quickly; "the rest is quite original."

There was a painful pause, and though I did not see the glance, I was conscious that the two women looked at each other with eyes unfavourable to me. They had divined that I did not appreciate Tom.

"Well, I will say good-morning," I said at last. "Many thanks for your kindness."

"Oh, it is no kindness, sir," said Polly. "I, I *hope* you like the picture. Mr. Bell has set *such* hopes on it. He thinks it will make our fortunes, and though I am not so hopeful as that, I *do* think that he should get a good price for it."

I looked at the thin face and the shabby gown, and said honestly that I hoped Mr. Bell *would* get a good price for it.

"I was thinking that some of the rich merchants might buy it," she continued; "there are so many of them in Melbourne, but Mr. Bell says that it is a national work, and that the trustees of the Public Library ought to take it. Do you think it would be of any use to offer it to them?"

"I don't know," said I, knowing right well. "They *might* buy it; but then, you see, they have commissioners in London who purchase for them."

"That is true," assented Polly; "and, as I tell Tom, a national work should be something about Australia, shouldn't it? But he says that Australia is mean and stupid, and that there is no romance about it. Of course High Art, you know, sir, is very exacting, and—but I am keeping you. I *wish* Mr. Bell had been here."

What could one say under such circumstances? The picture was only, in journalistic phrase, "worth a paragraph," but of what nature should that paragraph be? My duty was very plain. "We have seen a picture by Mr. T. Bell, *The Meeting of Cortez and Montezuma*. It is simply execrable." Had Mr. Bell himself, blatant, rubicund, and self-conceited, bored me for an hour with a sermon upon his own merits, I could have written such a paragraph with a savage joy; had caprice of fortune brought me accidentally before the daub, I could have justly consigned it to limbo, but—with the memory of that struggling household, that hopeful mother, that plucky Polly, "who was quite an artist,"—it was not to be thought of.

"I saw that picture of that fellow's," I said to my editor that evening. "It is—well—it is deuced bad, but the poor fellow—struggling beggar, don't you know?"

"Oh, confound him, yes," said my editor, with roseate smile. "Let him down easy, poor devil."

So I wrote my paragraph thus:—"We have been invited to inspect a picture by Mr. T. Bell. It represents *The Meeting of Cortez and Montezuma.* The Spanish conqueror stands, &c., &c., &c.; on the right, &c.; on the left, &c.; in the distance, &c. The subject of the painting has evidently been carefully considered by the artist, who has reproduced the scene as described by old Bernal Diaz with commendable accuracy. The figure of Marina is graceful, and the left nostril of the charger, &c., &c., &c. The painting will, we believe, be offered by Mr. Bell for sale in a few days."

The next day I was visited by Mr. Bell. He was a thin, consumptive, young man, with dirty nails, long hair, and a red beard.

"I have come to thank you for the notice of my picture, sir," he said, with a proud, constrained air; "but I am sorry that you did not see fit to mention the expression on the face of Montezuma."

"Ah!" said I.

"But no matter—you write, of course, according to your lights. Now, having so favourably reviewed my work, I have come to you, sir, to ask you to help me to sell it."

"Upon my word, Mr. Bell, I—"

"My dear sir, *you* are a writer, I am an artist. What need for more words. You will help me in this. In fact, just now, ha, ha!—you know Art is not appreciated here—well, in fact, I am rather poor—ha, ha!—and if that work could but be brought under the notice of men of taste, I am convinced, *convinced*, sir, that our little difficulties would be——." Here a fit of coughing cut him short.

"Mr. Bell," said I, "I will do anything I can to help you, but do not place your hopes of fortune upon the sale of that painting. It is" (my heart failed me)—"it is a subject unfamiliar to many. It does not appeal to public taste. It—in fact, there are reasons——"

"There are *no* reasons," said Mr. Bell, tossing his long hair. "Look here, sir; I must walk to Kew to give a lesson in drawing to a pawnbroker's daughter. I can't stop now. Will you come up to my studio and have a pipe this evening?"

"Thank you, Mr. Bell, but——"

"But you are engaged, I can understand. You have many——"

"No, no—I will come," I interposed, hastily, with a thought of the poor, proud fellow trudging to his accomplished pawnbroker's. "Expect me."

I went. We smoked, we drank Mrs. Polly's tea, we talked. He was the feeblest of mediocrities, and those dear, good women believed him a genius and worked for him, and admired him, and loved him.

"If Tom only had a chance," said Mrs. Bell the elder, stitching her stocking.

"This is such an envious place," said Mrs. Bell the younger, stippling her photograph.

Tom smoked, and talked Art, and raved about his Mission, and the Genius that was in him, and which (with a bang of his wasted hand upon the table) should come out of him—"by God, sir!"

I suppose we have all met with those unhappy souls who, only powerful enough to admire, are cursed with a desire to create. I have often thought what a work might be written upon the lives of unsuccessful men. It is easy to revere the genius who succeeds, though it is probable that the man whom the world delights to honour has suffered some heart-pangs; but, oh! with what infinite tenderness and pity should we regard those poor, unsuccessful ones, who, tasting all the agony of martyrdom, die without having grasped the crown!

Cortez and Montezuma steadily decreased in the estimation of all who saw it. I lied (Heaven forgive me) like a friend for the man. The truth was sufficiently plain. Mr. Bell would never be an artist. He was an enthusiast in art, that was all. He could but "copy" at the best. Some might think it manly and just to say, "Tom, you are an ambitious incapable. Your great picture is not worth twopence. You would earn a better living for your wife and mother if you were a bootmaker or a saddler." But I—seeing how gallantly the poor fellow strove to keep his silly noddle above water; how manfully he tramped through the mud to his vulgar patrons, and how sweetly these two good souls bore with the ill-temper caused by anxiety, sickness, and hope deferred—I did not, could not, wound them by the declaration of the cruel truth. I was an ass, dear Dives; pray, let me admit it! I brought merchants galore. I invited drapers (Mr. Stuckely, who had been "dresser" in Ribbonman's years ago, and now, being worth £20,000, bought pictures and went a-hunting on a fifty guinea horse which he couldn't ride). I besought Mr. Nosey (the ex-eating-house-keeper—the celebrated Welch rarebit-and-glass-of-ale-for-sixpence-man) to untie his purse-strings. I even got old Gripe out of his cobwebbed sanctum, and condescended to slap the contemptible hunks on the back in the hope of slapping some compassion into his sordid soul. In vain. Montezuma stared at us unmoved. "They *shall* buy you!" poor Bell would cry, shaking his fist at the unlucky monarch, but the vigour of the sentiment was its only recommendation.

Meanwhile, summer waned to autumn, autumn sank to winter, and Polly's fond eyes would fill with tears when the artist's hacking cough was heard on the stairs. What need to prolong the tale! The poor mediocrity died last week, with the daub that was to make him famous yet on the easel. Polly, the mother, and I buried him in Carlton Cemetery.

"He's happy now, poor dear," said Polly, amid her sobs, as we turned to leave the humble grave, "and *some* day they will appreciate his genius."

God bless the faithful women, they——

HOW THE CIRCUS CAME TO BULLOCKTOWN.

1. IN WHICH NEWS OF THE CIRCUS'S ARRIVAL PROMISES ESSENTIAL DISTRACTION.

When it became known that the Circus was coming to Bullocktown there was much excitement. Anything in the shape of amusement was so eagerly seized upon,—even a pound-sale was considered a joyous occasion,—that the news of a Circus within cooey, as one might say, almost took away the breath of the inhabitants.

The intelligence was brought by 'Arry, the mail-boy, who, riding to Grogmore and Brandyvale twice a week, had on his last journey fallen in with the Circus, camped (quite condescendingly) by the Muddy Waterholes. 'Arry's description of the regal magnificence of the proud proprietors of this travelling raree-show fired all the youth of the township, and juvenile Bullocktown burned for the arena. As has been hinted at, juvenile Bullocktown did not often get a chance to do anything but burn. Bullocktown did not offer any vast attractions to the itinerant showman, and even the Wizard Oil Man, daring beyond his compeers in exploring of "untrodden ways," drew the line at Quartzborough, and turned off to Grogmore by the way of St. Omer and Whiskey Flat. Two "performances" had indeed been given in the biggest parlour of the Royal Cobb, but they were not eminently successful. One of these was a "lecture," and the other an "entertainment." I witnessed both, and until I saw the Entertainment would have ventured to wager large sums that nothing in the way of amusement could be more dreary than the Lecture.

2. IN WHICH A "LECTURE" AND AN "ENTERTAINMENT" ARE DETAILED, AND ANNOTATED IN THE MARGIN MANY YEARS LATER BY ANOTHER HAND IN HALF-IMAGINED CONVERSATION.

THE "Siege of Sebastopol, with Illustrations," is, one would think, a subject which could be rendered interesting, if not instructive, but it wasn't. In the first place, the Illustrations were not all they might have been. A comic set of magic-lantern slides, representing Chinamen seized by sailors, rats entering the practicable mouths of sleeping miners, and marvellous men in red garments chasing anatomically alarming youths in blue, does not give one a very accurate idea of the Russian Campaign. Moreover, the lecturer was afflicted with what he was pleased to term "whisky in the hair," and was uncertain in his movements. Bullocktown grew bewildered when informed that, 'ere they saw the Eurilus, 28 guns,

Enjoy this traditional nineteenth-century literary digression.

Is any of this relevant? Can we just skip it?

Hang in there. It has its moments.

Are you sure of that?

What an age we live in that, to experience this kind of "lecture" today, we merely need to enter the words "truth movement" into a search engine. I can now watch at will poorly a hengagin' the Rooshian frigate Chokemoff, 181 guns (to the left Hadmiral Sir C. Napier standing on the foretops'le sheet block,) and were presented with a portrait of the Vale of Tempe, by moonlight, instead. Jack Harris, the son of the butcher, asked the lecturer in an unsophisticated way to "bring out his blank Sebastypool and get on," and when the lecturer wobbled in his speech, and hiccoughed solemnly during the Bombardment of Cronstadt, told him that "he'd never buy the child a new frock," and advised him to "knock off and have a smoke." Eventually the lecturer appealed to Longbow, who made a little speech, in which he stated that if his respected friend, Miss Burdett Coutts, could by any possibility have heard the ungentlemanly observations of Mr. Harris, she would "never get over it," as though *it* was a five-barred gate to be taken at a fly with a bad take off and an uncertain landing. Mr. Patrick Rafferty (Senior-constable Rafferty the *Quartzborough Chronicle* called him,) cut the gordian knot by locking Jack Harris in the stable until the "lecture" was concluded.

The "Entertainment" was given by Mr. and Mrs. Montacute, late of the Theatres Royal and Haymarket, Melbourne. The biggest table in the Royal

narrated video, slowed down and zoomed in to a particular part of the frame, as if this fuzzy footage proves something other than a profound wish that "zoom and enhance" were a real thing (which it isn't).

What's that got to do with this story?

If the author can follow a tangent for a page, then I can for a paragraph.

Things that have become less common in the last 142 years:

1. General interest in Sieges of Sevastopol (with a notable exception from 1941–1942)
2. Anglicising 'Sevastopol' with a 'b'
3. Magic lantern slides
4. References to 'Chinamen' (except in satire)
5. The need for quotes around Australia's 'born inhabitants'

Cobb was the stage, and Mrs. Montacute ran laughingly up a pair of steps on the left-hand to meet Mr. Montacute, who bounded gracefully from the vantage-ground of an inverted bucket, on the right. The curtain was a horsecloth, and the orchestra a piano, played by Tom Patterson, the overseer at Mount Melancholy, who had an ear for music, and who being in the township on a matter of post-and-rail fencing, most generously volunteered his services. I am afraid that the artistic position which poor Mr. and Mrs. Montacute occupied at the Theatres Royal and Haymarket had not been the most exalted one, but they did their best, and were received with rapturous applause. Indeed, when Mr. Montacute, clad severely in a dressing-gown of Longbow's (given him, of course, by his "intimate friend, the Marquis of Dooro,") rolled his eyes, and asked in a terrible voice, "Who has been opening oysters with my razor?" the peals of laughter were deafening. This was the more complimentary to the comic powers of Mr. Montacute for none of the "born inhabitants" of Bullocktown had ever seen an oyster in all their lives.

Things that have sadly disappeared in the last 142 years:

1. Anatomically alarming youths (as far as I can tell)
2. The phrase 'whiskey-in-the-hair'
3. Men who say 'hengagin"
4. Hiccoughs
5. Curtains made from horsecloth in amateur theatre
6. The Marquis of Dooro

Things we're sadly still stuck with 142 years later:

1. Bad amateur theatre

Really? You've resorted to listicles?

Give the public what they want.

3. IN WHICH THE CIRCUS ARRIVES (WITH A DECIDEDLY PURPLE TINGE), BEFORE A RICH METAPHOR IS APPLIED LIBERALLY WITH SOME LOVELY PROSE, AND THE WORD "PIEBALD" MAKES ITS FIRST APPEARANCE.

But to resume.

Riding along the bush road to Grogmore the day after the deliverance of 'Arry's budget, the traveller of the guide-books would have observed that the gum-trees were here and there "blazed" with posters.

While the pictures of the Brothers distorting their boneless limbs, the Machiavelian clown roaring with laughter at his own jests, and Mademoiselle Zepherina performing her feats in the Haute Ecole, were calculated to appal the stoutest beholder. By mid-day Bullocktown shook to its foundations—the Circus had arrived.

Most of us have seen that inexpressibly melancholy spectacle—a "Triumphal Entry by Circus Riders." We know the paint and powder, and long hair, and fillets, and piebald ponies, and big drums. We are familiar with the lovely damsels who are not lovely, and the spirited steeds that are not spirited, and the golden car that is not golden, and the sham and pretension of the whole business. We know how cold and wretched the Bounding Bricks look in their silk tights at mid-day, and how singularly bony are the Boneless Brothers. We sympathise with the dusty team of sixteen creams that comport themselves with such preposterous affectation of suddenly making for their native pastures, and dragging at their fiery heels the fragments of the Triumphal Car. We observe even the bulged and blackened stocking knee of the Famed Equestrienne, and bethink us how many times it has knelt in vain to the Murderous Marauder who, bestriding three

BUNCOMBE'S IMPERIAL YANKO-AMERICAN CIRCUS!

THE MOST COMPLETE STUD IN THE AUSTRALIAS!

THE BONELESS BROTHERS OF BLAZING BELT!

FEATS IN THE HAUTE ECOLE!

MADEMOISELLE ZEPHERINA, THE FAIRY EQUESTRIENNE!

MR. STANISLAUS BUNCOMBE, THE MACHIAVELIAN CLOWN!

The Pavillion is fitted up in a tasteful style, and conducted in such a manner as to ensure the attention of many who never go to theatrical amusements.

Admittance.– **Box Seats 1/6. Pit 1s. General 6d.**

D&D. LETTERPRESS, Printers, Albury-Wadonga.

steeds at once, would fain bear off the pearl of the Haute Ecole across his triple saddle-bow. All this we have seen, and have commented on in our various methods,–some parsonically, with hints of burnings in store for the abandoned folk; some cynically, as betokening a condition of sham and humbug typical of much in humanity; some kindly and cheerily, with knowledge of good-fellowship and friendship displayed among these hard-working holiday-makers that might put better-dressed and more respectable people to shame. But I doubt if it has fallen to the lot of many of us to see the strange sight which this eighth wonder of Bullocktown presented when contrasted with its surroundings. The sordid little wooden stores, the grey grim gum trees, the staring public-house, the unmetalled roads, the dispiriting "newness" of the whole place, and in the midst of this procession of unreal heroes, mock marauders, motley clowns, and pasteboard knights-in-armour.

Three times did the Circus encircle the township, and then it coiled itself gradually into the back-yard of the Royal Cobb, to be seen of men no more until night. By-and-by certain cadaverous, greasy-haired people came into Longbow's bar, and condescendingly drank with the inhabitants. In the bar congregated at once the rank and fashion of the township.

Mr. Bluffem was there, also Mrs. Bluffem, called by her affectionate husband, "Ize Betzy," and popularly known as "Bluffem's Bet." Flash Harry, the coach driver, was there, in breeches of appalling tightness, and loose spurs that jingled highwayman-like as he walked. There was also little Potkins, the owner of the adjoining run of Marshmallows, and numerous horses, "mokes" as their owners termed them, were hanging at various degrees of neck-extension, to the rings on the Royal Cobb verandah post.

By-and-by the Boneless Brothers, attended by an admiring crowd of township children, marked out a sort of free selection on a piece of waste ground, between M'Taggart the blacksmith's, and the school-house, and in the course of an hour or so a wondrous erection of poles and canvas to which the tent of the Fairy Peri Barron (so celebrated in Eastern story) was but a shanty in comparison, rose into being. On the top of this canvas mushroom flew in the hot wind an enormous flag. The "Circus" had become a fact.

4. IN WHICH BULLOCKTOWN PREPARES FOR THE OPENING OF THE SHOW, MOSTLY BY DRINKING COPIOUSLY AND, IN SYMPATHY, THE TEXT BEGINS TO STUMBLE.

DURING the afternoon the world and his wife trooped into Bullocktown. Stockmen were abundant, and riding their own horses for the day, behaved with that reckless disregard of life and limb which characterises stockmen on such occasions.

The yard of the Three Posts presented a curious appearance. Hans Kolsen, the "cranky shepherd," was expatiating on the mystery of the Mallee to a crowd of bearded fellows, who alternately ridiculed and "shouted" for him. Sandy M'Donald fought a pitched battle with Andy O'Brien; and that one-armed hero, old Neil Gow, the boundary rider ("shepherd-ranger" he loved to term himself,) bent pewter pots and held up strong men in his teeth, and achieved other feats for which he had become celebrated throughout the district. The fiddles struck up fast and furious in the "long room," the tobaccoed brandy circulated freely, and before sundown had the traveller before mentioned paused for an instant at the bridge, he could not have failed to have come to the conclusion to have come to the conclusion that Bullocktown was in the primary stage of intoxication.

The circus was to open at half-past seven o'clock, and shortly before that hour the crowd around the Royal Cobb increased in density. Mr. Patrick Rafferty—his whiskers blazing with a sense of duty—exerted himself to the utmost to preserve order, and with patriotic disregard of expense dressed himself defiantly in full uniform. The avenues and passages of the Royal Cobb—not too many, nor too wide—were choked with enthralled inhabitants. The Equestrienne was eating in an adjoining apartment. Rumour with its thousand tongues even hinted that Stanislaus Buncombe himself had, with Machiavelian Clownishness, ordered steak and onions. Great thought! The dish rose in the estimation of Bullocktown from that hour.

The violet darkness of a moonless summer night had fallen on the tent when the canvas flap was lifted to admit the multitude. Prices did not rule high—one shilling to the pit, one shilling and sixpence to the boxes, and sixpence to all other parts of the house, were the advertised charges; and Bullocktown, on pleasure bent, thronged to the pit. It was rumoured that three shillings had been charged in Quartzborough for a seat in that locality, and that so high were the notions of the circus proprietors, that but for the necessity of "spelling" their horses they would not have performed in Bullocktown at all, but gone straight to Grogmore. It was pleasant to see how Bullocktown appreciated the honour done it, and lavished its shillings on pit seats.

The aristocrats—that is to say, Little Potkins Tom Patterson, Dick Stevens of the Gash, and other wealthy squatters, occupied the boxes, and tapped their boots with the thong-ends of their Sunday riding whips with much dignity. Meerschaum pipes obtained about this part of the house, and young

Sholto (learning colonial experience,) who was generally supposed to devote his existence to the colouring of these articles, had mounted the most gigantic specimen in his collection in pure honour of the occasion. Tom Patterson—the rogue—ogled the two township belles, and even dared to cast the eye of flirtation on pretty Mrs. Ballantine, the poundkeeper's lately-achieved bridge. Potkins sucked the German-silver head of his whip, and looked knowing, while Stevens, who was in sush— "society" when in town, leant agggaainst the posht and ass-assumed a blasé air.

A moment of ankshusss expectation, and the Macky, the Machiiiva, the m-m-Machiavelian One himself lept inta the ring.

5. IN WHICH, ALTHOUGH STANISLAUS—CIRCUS OWNER AND CLOWN—BOMBS, AND HICCOUGHS BECOME HICCUPS, MADEMOISELLE ZEPHERINA, HER SAILOR-LOVER, AND THE BONELESS BROTHERS NEVERTHELESS BRING THE HOUSE DOWN. FOR THE COMPLETE STORY, REFER TO COMMENT FROM OUR REGULAR COLUMNIST FROM *THE AUSTRALASIAN*, 20 AUGUST 1870.

THE SKETCHER.

By Marcus Clarke.

I BELIEVE that the Machiavelian One was a good clown. I have seen his Memoirs penned by my versatile hic-et-ubique friend Bob Jingle—bound in green covers with a pensive portrait of the humourist himself on the back of it, and been alarmed at his violent predilection for jesting. I am willing—even now—to believe that the M.O. has turned fifteen double somersaults in succession, peeling and eating an orange during the process, and that as a "jumpist," so to speak, he is without a rival. But candour compels me to admit, on this occasion, he was not sparkling. I have heard funnier jests than those that fell from his Machiavelian lips, and have witnessed acrobatic feats quite as dangerous as those which horrified the Bullocktown public on this particular evening. But perhaps the day's journey had fatigued him, or perhaps—and this supposition is not an improbable one—he did not care about wasting his best jokes upon a Bullocktown audience.

It was well that he did not, for from the instant he entered a storm of noises shook the canvas. All the powers of bullock-driving badinage—seldom elegant—were put in force to drive him from the ring. The good folks thought he was the fool he feigned to be and laughed at him, not with him! When the ring-master—chosen, I imagine, for that exalted office on account of the peculiar breadth and beauty of his whiskers—lashed the clown, the audience solemnly applauded him, and when poor Stanislaus, in ecstasies of melancholy laughter, upset and trampled upon the ring-master, the audience cried "Shame!" at the unmanly action. It was evident that they regarded the jester as the one serious blot upon the amusement of the evening!

This being the unexpected conclusion, haste was made to bring in the Equestrienne, who was graciously received. Mademoiselle Zepherina sat gracefully on the tail end of her fiery charger—a Roman-nosed animal of sedate and wise appearance who seemed to be rather ashamed of his capers and caparisons—stood upon one leg and smiled beamingly, and leapt through hoops and bounded over silk scarfs (falling upon her knees with tremendous accuracy) until Bullocktown would have died for her fair sake to a man. Three times was she compelled to re-enter and kiss her fingers in acknowledgement of the homage of her subjects, and in the last grand act, where her sailor-lover (having torn off his trousers and flung them to the winds,) stripped off so many costumes during his rapid flight that blushing matrons, unused to daring acts of equitation, wondered alarmedly how deep he meant to go, the applause was deafening. The lover, peeled to the last tight, waved his breathless thanks, and sank exhausted on the pad of his foaming piebald. As the flap closed on the pair the tumult was a hurricane, tempered by hiccups.

At this entrancing instant a pattering sound was heard. One of those violent and sudden showers which sometimes burst upon up-country townships was about to descend upon the tent. The ringmaster paused in the midst of a whip crack, and the Machiavelian jester had need of all his diplomacy to assume a jocular appearance. All faces turned simultaneously to the roof, and some half-dozen men were observed to rush past the ticket-taker and vanish into the now cloudy night. The entrance of the Boneless Brothers recalled us to revelry. No event of less importance could have availed to do so.

The boneless pair were certainly very startling. The way in which they defied the anatomists, by putting their heads where their feet ought to be, and tying themselves into knots of the most gristly description, was perfectly perplexing. Longbow—who amongst other professions owned that of a surgeon—said that the cartilaginous formation was extraordinary, only equalled, indeed, by that of his poor dear friend, Lord Herbert of Cherbury, who had (upon Longbow's soul) the most remarkable development of muscle ever vouchsafed to man. But when the B.B. bent themselves into a triumphal arch, of which their heads were the keystone, and walked upon their hands twice round the arena, even Longbow felt compelled conscientiously to admit that Lord Herbert of Cherbury was, in comparison, cartilaginously nowhere.

As the brothers rose, empurpled from this feat, a hideous yell resounded, and the canvas, after swaying ominously, bulged into the centre.

The tin-hoop chandelier, with its wreath of flaming tallow dips, dropped rattling into the "boxes," and amid a wild shriek of dismay the whole fabric collapsed upon us. Those merry fellows outside had cut the ropes!

6. IN WHICH A KNIFE COMES IN HANDY, FIGURATIVELY AND LITERALLY, AS A CLOWN EXPERIENCES A NUMBER OF EMOTIONS, THE VITAL FLUIDS OF COLONIES REMAINS CONTAINED, AND THE SEQUENCE OF WORDS WITHIN THE SECTION ALGORITHMICALLY RECALL THE BARD, FOLLOWING THEIR TRIP THROUGH THE DELETIONIST.

THE cry of women pierced the canvas, and a running accompaniment of strong language testified that male Bullocktown was not at ease.

It is not a good thing to be suddenly swamped in a sea of dusty canvas, and for a few moments suffocation seemed imminent. Longbow, however, who was next to me, suggested a remedy.

"I've got a knife in my trousers-pocket," said he, in semi-stifled tones, "and if you can get it out we'll cut the canvas. *My* arms are immovable."

Painfully conscious of the immediate and oppressive presence of "Ize Betzy," I made shift to grasp the desired weapon, and plunged it into the blinding mass above me. With a sound like that emitted by a tearing sheet, the tent split in sunder, and we wriggled out. The momentary glimpse we got of the chaos out of which we had escaped was not calculated to reassure us. The centre tent-pole alone remained. Grimly upright, it protruded from a heaving desert of dirty white canvas, upon which the gathering rain fell patteringly. This canvas was here and there bulged with heads and pinnacled with feet.

Indistinct growlings and groanings escaped from it, and at the slit from which we had emerged peered one forlorn face.

It was that of Stanislaus Buncombe himself.

Longbow extended the hand which had been pressed so many times in friendship by F. M. the

Duke of Wellington, and dragged the Machiavelian One gasping to air.

"Oh my!" said he, "here's an almighty slide."

He spoke truly. It *was* an almighty slide, and looked like nothing so much as a dirty avalanche that had lost its way in a London fog, except perhaps a monster bundle of clothes split on their course to a Titanic wash.

The clown surveyed the scene with emotion, but at last the driving rain, filling his clownish pockets with water, compelled him to cease meditation. Around us—on the edge of this desert of overturned circus-riding, were several figures who appeared from their gestures to be on the point of expiring in convulsions of laughter. These were the merry dogs who had perpetrated this exquisite jest. Stanislaus seized upon two of these as volunteers, and borrowing the knife that had done such good service, he rapidly cut the cords that bound the canvas to the tent-pegs.

For an instant it appeared as though the vast sheet would be twisted into a ball by the struggles of the creatures beneath, but Buncombe catching one end of it, and Neil Gow the other, they "skinned" it from the corporate body beneath. Rending as it ran, into its various sections, the emblazoned tent was pulled from the *élite* of Bullocktown. Squirming, struggling, gasping, fighting, there lay the best blood of the township, the human bottles that held what Daw, the editor of the *Quartzborough Gazette*, so euphoniously termed the "vital fluid of the colonies."

Despite all one's knowledge of their misery and discomfort, one could not forbear a laugh at the appearance of the "audience." It was as though we had overturned a huge stone that covered a snug family of earth worms. Though not a head was visible, I never fully realised the truth of the saying "that man is but a forked radish with head fantastically carved" until then. Stanislaus was a modest man, and he turned away his face with a gasp of dismay.

In a few minutes, however, all were upright, and then was confusion worse confounded than before. Several friendly fights, began under the obscurity of the canvas, were concluded above ground. Women wept over crushed bonnets and torn dresses. "Ize Betzy" urged her lord to execute instant vengeance upon the whole troupe of circus-riders, and catching sight of poor Stanislaus, made at him like a lioness. Not all the diplomacy of Machiavel was equal to the occasion, and feebly uttering "My good woman!" the proprietor of the Yanko-American Circus turned and fled. "I'll good woman you," screamed Mrs. Bluffem. "Wait a minute, you dog! Wait a minute."

But Stanislaus had no such intention. Bounding over the fallen patriarchs of the village, he ran like a deer for the Royal Cobb, and reaching his bedroom a hand's-breadth in advance of "Ize Betzy," locked the door, vanished from view. Mrs. Bluffem, foiled in her vengeance, and wet to the skin, screamed "Fire!" at the top of her voice, and, falling into strong convulsions, was only to be got round by still stronger brandy and water, administered scalding hot in the biggest tumbler the house afforded.

7. IN WHICH WE MEET THE MYSTERIOUS BEAST (THE LONELY GENIUS WHO WILL NOT BE "ROKED") AND THE KNIFE-SWALLOWING BOY (WHOM YOU WOULD BE ILL-ADVISED TO FIND YOURSELF ON THE WRONG SIDE OF). MUST EVERYTHING IN THE STORY DEGENERATE INTO A RIOT?

BY-AND-BY, however, the first flavour of alarm having gone off, it was found that after all the affair was a most excellent jest, and merited drinks all round. So more dark brandy was consumed, and Bullocktown agreed in the parlour, passages, and what-not of the Royal Cobb, that it had not enjoyed itself so much for years, and that the true way to see a circus performance was to cut the ropes of the tent at the earliest opportunity.

This conclusion having been amicably arrived at, and the Yanko-Americans pledged bottle deep in liquor—which they drank suddenly and silently, as though they were not quite satisfied at the hilarity of their hosts—it was discovered that there was yet more excitement. A Mysterious Beast and a Knife-swallowing Boy were exhibiting in a small booth which had escaped the general overthrow, and sixpence was the price of admission.

The Mysterious Beast was certainly very mysterious. He was a clean-shaved melancholy animal, with a collar of grey fur round his neck, and a chain round his body. He sat on his hind legs in a corner, and moaned plaintively, shaking his miserable head from side to side as though he would exclaim against the wickedness of the world and the intolerable vanity of circus-riders. The only creature I had ever seen that resembled him in the slightest degree was a worthy Pastor at Aberdeen that preached there to me one Sabbath upon "Blawin' 'oop the trumpet i' the fool moon," and did so with just such a woebegone expression.

It was evident that the Mysterious Beast was weighed down by the consciousness of his mystery. He felt the loneliness of genius.

The Knife-swallowing Boy was, however, of a most cheerful character. He was stupendously fat. (I am indeed of opinion that he was in training for greatness in that profession, and burned to eclipse Lambert). His eyes were of a pale blue, and his cheeks a sodden white. His tights were stretched to their utmost, and rolls of adipose tissue hung down over his spangled boots. If he swallowed nothing but knives, cutlery must have agreed with him wonderfully.

He commenced operations by a snack of pebbles. Handing round some good sized pieces of quartz upon a plate, he informed us that he was in the habit of consuming these delicacies in prodigal profusion, and that he found they were eminently satisfying and agreeable. Having said this he swallowed—or seemed to swallow—five or six in rapid succession, and made a low bow. The audience thrilled with delight, and one gentleman, in an ecstasy of admiration, swore with surprising energy for several minutes.

The boy, however, took this compliment as his evident due, and disdainfully spat into his hand. A lean man in the corner, who acted as showman to this exhibition, said as solemnly as if he really believed it, "He eats ten o' them every morning afore breakfast. It is supposed by physicians that the flints striking fire with the steel, enables him to better digest this remarkable repast." The boy sniffed contemptuously at this, and pretended not to know that everybody was looking at him.

"He will now swallow a sword," said the lean man. "'And it round Master Merryweather! 'and it round!"

So the sword was 'anded round, and everybody felt it and weighed it, looked knowingly over it, and tried if it would go into the handle, and if it was real steel, and winked their eyes mysteriously, or affected to pass it by with a placid smile, as though they had seen it habitually from boyhood, and knew the man who made it.

During this process I got a little closer to the boy, and observed that he was standing on a platform, around the bottom of which was a legend to this effect:—

"JOHN LAMBTON MERRYWEATHER,

"AGE, 14½ YEARS, BORN IN THE COUNTY OF GRANT. HE SWALLOWS KNIVES, SWORDS, AND ALL SORTS OF OLD IRON. HE EATS PEBBLES, AND IS PASSIONATELY FOND OF CHALK.

"AUSTRALIANS!

"PATRONISE NATIVE TALENT!

"Price 6d."

By the time I had read this over, the sword had been returned, and the swallow was about to commence. Stretching his legs very wide apart, the boy flung back his head until the Adam's-apple in his throat protruded in a dangerous manner, and then holding the sword very straight in the air, he allowed it to slide into his gullet. To the horror of all of us, the hilt rested upon his teeth, and the blade consequently fifteen inches deep into his stomach. After remaining in this position for an instant, the boy rapidly stretched out his arms, and the lean man, mounting swiftly on a chair, dexterously drew the weapon from its human sheath, and handed round the reeking blade to be admired.

During the awe-stricken silence which followed upon this feat, a wild shriek was heard. It proceeded from little Potkins, who, tormenting the Mysterious Beast, had been bitten severely for his pains.

"Go it!" says the lean man. "Wot der want to hirritate him for?"

"I wasn't irritating him," says Potkins.

"Yes yer were; I sor yer," says the boy. "You was a rokin' of him. Yer carn't expect beasts to be quiet when folks rokes 'em."

Flash Harry scented a riot.

The boy solemnly

a
d
v
a
n
c
e
d.

"Shut up, you young quartz-crusher," said he. "Who asked for your opinion?"

"Hold on my pipkin," he said. "Wait till I get up with yer, and we'll see whose quartz'ill get

c r u s h e d ."

"Come on young stoneworks," says Harry.

"Roll up here and show yer muscle."

The crowd parted like water, and in another minute Harry and the boy were at it hammer and tongs. I'll do Harry the justice to say that he fought well, but he was nowhere against the boy. That corpulent infant had been apparently bred to the science of self-defence, and the precision with which he planted his fatal left upon the nose of the horsebreaker was—as Longbow declared—beautiful to see.

After the third blow of this sort, which induced Harry's nose to spurt burstingly beneath the fat fist, as though it had been a suddenly-quashed gooseberry, the fight was virtually over, and the boy withdrew. Harry was removed by Potkins, and harmony seemed again restored, when a terrible accident was found to have taken place—the Mysterious Beast had vanished. Taking advantage of the confusion, the captive had escaped. It would be "roked" no more.

The lean man was violently wroth at this, and preposterously accusing Neil Gow of having concealed the marvellous animal about his person, was promptly knocked head over heels by that gigantic worthy.

The boy came to the rescue, and the row—for it deserves no better name—became fiercely general. The booth was uprooted, and the knife-swallower ran some danger of annihilation. But help was nigh. The circus-riders came down upon us in a compact mass, and cut into us like a wedge. Hemmed in and separated from our companions, Longbow and I surrendered at discretion, but the others, madly drunk, fought until they could fight no longer. The place where the Circus had been was the arena of one of the freest fights I remember. The circus men were terribly sober, and in most unpleasant "condition." They had evidently made up their minds to avenge the destruction of their tent, and they did so most completely. I did not see much of the combat, but in about half-an-hour the Yanko-Americans returned, and ordered whiskies hot. Their coats were torn, and their faces badly cut, but not a Bullocktown man showed in their wake. One of the Bounding Brothers was kind enough to ask me for a light, and I took the opportunity of enquiring what had become of my companions. "Guess we kinder squelched 'em," said he. And I guess they kinder had, for not another resident showed his nose that evening. Having thus celebrated their victory, the Yanko-Americans began to look about them for amusement, and, strange to say, they found it ready at their hand.

8. IN WHICH A PAIR OF WOWSERS AND THEIR WIVES ARE SUBJECTED TO THE TRICKERIES OF THE YANKO-AMERICANS. THIS SECTION OF THE STORY IS KINDLY SPONSORED BY THE BREWERY OF BARCLAY, PERKINS & CO., OF PARK-STREET, SOUTHWARK[1], MAKERS OF FINE BEERS, ALES AND TWO-PENNIES.

Curiously enough that very evening had arrived at the Royal Cobb a teetotal lecturer whose eloquence had formerly moved Bullocktown to repentance and sodawater. The name of this distinguished man was Barclay, and he had with him a teetotal friend, who, by one of those laughable coincidences which so often occur in life,

---

1 To the Brewery of Barclay, Perkins and Co., in Park-street, Southwark, has attached a greater celebrity, from its great extent. It may be inspected by a letter of introduction to the proprietors; and a great number of the foreigners of distinction who visit the metropolis avail themselves of such permission. The Brewery and its appurtenances occupy about twelve acres of ground, immediately adjoining Bankside, and extending from the land-arches of Southwark Bridge nearly half of the distance to those of London Bridge. Within the Brewery walls is said to be included the site of the famous Globe Theatre, "which Shakespeare has bound so closely up with his own history." In an account of the neighbourhood, dated 1795, it is stated that "the passage which led to the Globe Tavern, of which the playhouse formed a part, was, till within these few years, known by the name of Globe-alley, and upon its site now stands a large storehouse for Porter." We are inclined to regard this evidence merely as traditional. However, the last Globe Theatre was taken down about the time of the Commonwealth; and so late as 1720, Maid-lane (now called New Park-street), of which Globe-alley was an offshoot, was a long, straggling place, with ditches on each side, the passage to the houses being over little bridges with little garden-plots before them (Strype's Stow). *

was named Perkins.[2] The two were sworn friends,

---

2 Early in the last century there was a Brewery in Southwark, comparatively very small; it then belonged to a Mr. Halsey, who, on retiring from it with a large fortune, sold it to the elder Mr. Thrale; he became Sheriff of Surrey and M.P. for Southwark, and died in 1758. About this time the produce of the Brewery was 30,000 barrels a year. Mr. Thrale's son succeeded him, and found the Brewery so profitable and secure an income, that, although educated to other tastes and habits, he did not part with it; yet the Brewery, through Thrale's unfortunate speculation elsewhere, was at one time, according to Mrs. Thrale, £130,000 in debt, besides borrowed money; but in nine years every shilling was paid. Thrale was the warm friend of Dr. Johnson, who, from 1765 to the brewer's death, lived partly in a house near the Brewery, and at his villa at Streatham. Before the fire at the Brewery, in 1832, a room was pointed out, near the entrance gateway, which the Doctor used as a study. In 1781 Mr. Thrale died, and his executors, of whom Johnson was one, sold the Brewery to David Barclay, junior, then the head of the banking firm of Barclay and Co., for the sum of £135,000. "We are not here," said Johnson, on the day of the sale, "to sell a parcel of boilers and vats, but the potentiality of growing rich beyond the dreams of avarice." While on his tour to the Hebrides, Johnson mentioned that Thrale paid £20,000 a year to the revenue, and that he had four vats, each of which held 1600 barrels, above 1000 hogsheads. David Barclay placed in the brewing firm his nephew from America, Robert Barclay, who became of Bury Hill; and Mr. Perkins, who had been in Mr. Thrale's establishment—hence the firm of "Barclay and Perkins." Robert Barclay was succeeded by his son, Charles Barclay, who sat in Parliament for Southwark; and by his sons and grandsons. Forty years since, the Brewery was of great extent; in 1832 a great portion of the old premises was destroyed by fire, but was rebuilt, mostly of iron, stone, and brick. The premises extend from New Park-street, southward, through Park-street, both sides of which are the Brewery buildings, connected by a light suspension bridge; to the right is the vast brewhouse and principal entrance. There are extensive ranges of malt-houses extending northward, with a wharf to Bankside. From the roof of nearly the middle of the premises may be had a bird's-eye view of the whole. *

and hunted in couples. The low-backed shandry-dan—half buggy, half go-cart—in which they rode was well known in the district, and with its full freight of lecturers and lecturers' wives, had been dubbed: "Barclay and Perkins' Entire."[3] This shandry-dan was now resting in Longbow's back-yard, and the four eschewers of the evil of strong drink seated in Longbow's best parlour.

Mrs. Barclay was a tall, thin, and aristocratic lady; Mrs. Perkins was podgy, short, and plebeian. Mrs. Barclay was severe in demeanour; Mrs. Perkins was merry withal. Mrs. Barclay read serious books; Mrs. Perkins affected novels of the Percy B. St. John type. They both, however, agreed on the subject of alcoholic liquors; for the matter of that they might have been twinned in teetotalism. It was rumoured that Mrs. Perkins had been heard to express more than friendly admiration for Mr. Barclay, and that Mrs. Barclay had owned to a tender respect for the noble character of Mr. Perkins. As for Barclay and Perkins, they were like brothers. To see them, you would think Cato and Hortensius were not

3 Before the year 1730 the malt liquors most in use in London were ale, beer, and a drink called two-penny. It was then customary to call for a pint or tankard of half-an-half, *i.e.*, half ale, half beer, or half ale, and half two-penny. In course of time it also became practice to call for a pint or tankard of three-thirds, *i.e.*, ale, beer, and two-penny; for this the publican had the trouble of going to three casks, and turning three cocks for one pint of liquor. To avoid this inconvenience, a brewer named Harwood conceived of the idea of making a liquor which should partake of the united flavour of ale, beer, and two-penny; he did so, and succeeded to a miracle, calling it Harwood's *Entire,* and it was a very nourishing and hearty liquor, and supposed to be very suitable for porters and other working people, it obtained the name of "Porter", which is retained to this day, as also the word "Entire" which we can see daily in Barclay and Perkins' Entire. +

more unselfishly affectionate.

Plump upon this happy quartet did Stanislaus Buncombe, creeping down the passage in mortal terror of "Ize Betzy," fall.

"A thousand pardons."

"Pray, come in," said Mr. Perkins, with a sigh. "It may chance that we win another soul to grace."

This blessed utterance was heard by the troupe, and expecting fun, they blocked the doorway.

"Come in, me Keristian friends," says Barclay, with a sigh that seemed to rend his vitals. "Oh! Come in!"

Mr. Perkins in the meanwhile addressed himself to Stanislaus, with a smile,

"Do you drink, sir?"

"Thank you," says the bewildered Machiavel, expectant of liquor, "I do."

"I thought so," returned Mr. Perkins, throwing himself back in his chair, "Dorothy, my dear, just look at this unhappy man!"

Mrs. Perkins tittered (in a pious way) and looked. "Is he not a miserable spectacle?" asked Perkins, with deep sorrow in his tones. "Oh why do the heathen thus furiously rage together?"

Stanislaus began to see how the land lay, and with Machiavelian sharpness, winked at his joyous band. "Ize Betzy" had departed, and he felt himself a man again. "My dear sir," he said, "do you know that your teetotal cordials are more pernicious than any quantity of ardent spirits?"

Barclay waved his hand to Perkins, as who should say, "here is another benighted heathen. Hark at him!"

"I was not aware of it," says Perkins, "I have heard the argument many times before. It is a favourite one with the children of Beeelial."

"It's a fact," says Stanislaus. "Mr. Longbow, bring me some stomach bitters."

Longbow brought them.

"Drink this," said he, "and tell me your candid opinion."

Perkins drank and handed the bottle to Barclay.[4] The bitters were good, for the holy men smiled a pleasant smile.

"It is comforting," said Barclay.

Stanislaus pretended to be astonished, and drank himself. "Upon my word," he cried, "it is not bad. I half begin to believe your doctrines."

"Sit down, my friend," cried Barclay, "and I shall expound them yet further unto thee."

"The ladies," says Stanislaus, "if they will forgive a poor player; but discussion is weary, and—may I suggest lemonade?"

Mrs. Barclay iced herself at once, but Mrs. Perkins bowed a gracious assent, and the lemonade was brought.

I have not now space to give the sermon that was preached by the pair, but it was a good one, and one of these days I may repeat it. Suffice it

---

4 The water used for brewing is pumped up by a steam-engine through a large iron main, which passes under the malt warehouses, and leads to the "liquor-backs," two cast-iron cisterns, on columns, reaching an elevation of some 40 feet. By this means the establishment may be supplied with water for brewing to the extent of a hundred thousand gallons daily. There is on the premises an Artesian well 367 feet deep; but its water, on account of its low temperature, is principally used for cooling the beer in hot weather. The machinery is worked throughout the Brewery by steam. The furnace-shaft is 19 feet below the surface, and 110 feet above; and, by its great height, denotes the situation of this gigantic establishment among the forest of Southwark chimneys. The malt is deposited in enormous bins, each of the height or depth of an ordinary three-storied house. The rats are kept in check by a standing army of cats, who are regularly fed and maintained. The malt is conveyed to be ground in tin buckets upon an endless leather band ("Jacob's Ladder"); and thus carried to the height of 60 or 70 feet, in the middle of the Great Brewhouse, built entirely of iron and brick, and lighted by eight large and lofty windows. *

here to say that we all sat down and listened, and that the two holy men applied themselves vigorously to the stomach bitters between whiles. Talking was dry work. The evening waned, and Stanislaus gallantly ordered more lemonade. We drank a good deal of lemonade, and then the ladies retired to a sort of cock-loft bedchamber suite of three rooms that were built upon the upper storey.

"The bitters are empty," said Stanislaus. "Another bottle. Your discourse has impressed me."

So more bitters were brought, and more lemonade, and presently I began to feel unaccountably drowsy.

A glance through the open door explained the mystery. Longbow, doubtless by that villain Stanislaus' directions, had been putting gin into the lemonade, and brandy into the cordial!

What need for further explanation? Perkins began to wander in his speech, and Barclay to get unsteady on his legs. Babbling peacefully of teetotalism, they were soon as happily drunk as the most confirmed toper of us all. Stanislaus, triumphant, called for a "health," and filling up a cordial glass to the brim with brandy, he handed it to Perkins.

"Water for ever!" cried he.

"Waw, waw, water for—egh!" says Perkins, draining the brandy, with a dreadful splutter, and suddenly awakening to the consciousness of the trick that had been played upon him. "Why you ouv, ouv, villain, I'm t-t-tight!" Here speech failed him, and he fell exhausted on the carpet.

Then came our task to convey them to bed. With wondrous exercise of mechanical ingenuity, we bore them upstairs, and opening the doors of their rooms, bundled him in and retreated. But when half way down the stairs a wild cry arose, and two white figures rushed at each other on the landing.

"Jeerusalem!" says the leader of the Yanko-Americans, "but we've put 'em into wrong rooms!"

It was even so. Mr. Barclay had invaded the chamber of Mrs. Perkins, and Mr. Perkins that of Mrs. Barclay. 'Twas like a scene from Smollett. The two ladies, each thinking that she had discovered her husband's infidelity, flew at each other with deadly fury. Barclay, holding on by the bannister, denounced them both, but Perkins, too drunk to stand, clapped his hands feebly, and said with the last flicker of expiring sense, "Gug-go it Kak! Kak-Karoline!"

Who is it says that nothing is more gratifying to the gods than the spectacle of a good man struggling with adversity?

But I am not a god, so let me draw the veil.

THOMMO'S CAR RESORATION

HOLDENS, FORDS, &C., &C., &C.

7 BIMBIL ST, ALBION.
(OPPOSITE THE "RED GARTER").

ASK FOR KEITH.

BOTOX

THE widest selection of the latest injectables, dermal abrasions laser therapies, cellulite erasure, & fat loss techniques. *PRICES AVAILABLE ON REQUEST.* Discounts available for multiple treatments.

MEN!

WE CATER FOR YOUR NEEDS TOO: PROTEIN POWDERS, "VITAMIN" INJECTIONS, ENERGY BOOSTERS AVAILABLE ON REQUEST.

Smiley & Associates.
12/80 Wickham Terrace, Brisbane.
Other locations throughout South-East Queensland.

A NEW, BETTER YOU, CREATED ON DEMAND.

Protect Yourself Against Home Intruders

STRANGERS want to break into your home and steal your stuff. Arm yourself with a DVR security system connected with CCTV security systems, enabling you to record what the CCTV cameras see, and play it back at a later date.

FROM COMPUTER, SMARTPHONE, OR TABLET.

F. FULSOME & CO.,
99 ANN-STREET, BRISBANE.

Keep undesirable people away from you, where they cannot be seen.

http://protectyourselffromtheother.com.au

WARNING.

HM GOVERNMENT'S MANDATORY DATA RETENTION LEGISLATION HAS BEEN PASSED. NOW IS YOUR LAST CHANCE TO PROTECT YOURSELF.

OUR exclusive *FUSION PARANOIA* engine encrypts all your digital connections and provides you with an anonymous IP to protect your privacy in every digital interaction from end to end.

Our state of the art, multi-layered security offers advanced privacy protection.

USING VPN TUNNELLING. SERVICES OPERATE AT THE TCP/IP INTERFACE LEVEL, WHICH MEANS ALL OF YOUR APPLICATIONS WILL BE SECURED, NOT JUST YOUR WEB BROWSER.

DOWNLOAD OUR TRIAL SOFTWARE TODAY.

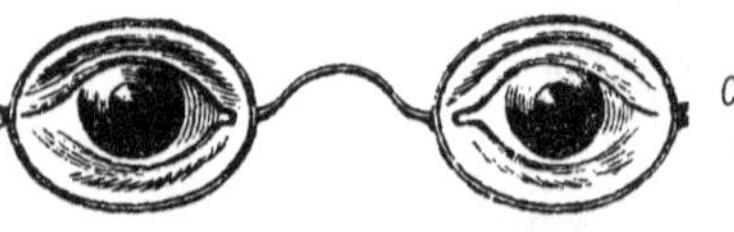

NO CREDIT CARD REQUIRED. EVER.

HTTP://WWW.ASKFORKEITH.IO

GENSYS LOGISTICS

(LATE WATTSWORTH SECURITY SERVICE).

OFTEN ACCUSED, NEVER CONVICTED.

PROVIDING TRUSTWORTHY SECURITY AND TACTICAL SUPPORT FOR THE CROWN AND PRIVATE SECTOR.

Our famous *NO-QUESTIONS-ASKED*, no-leaks policy ensures your government department or corporation's motives will not be subjected to frivolous public scrutiny.

ISOLATED LOCATIONS OUR SPECIALTY.

THIRD SPEAKER BOX, PLATFORM TEN. (ASK FOR KEITH).

Roma-Street, **BRISBANE.**

THE POOR WRITER.

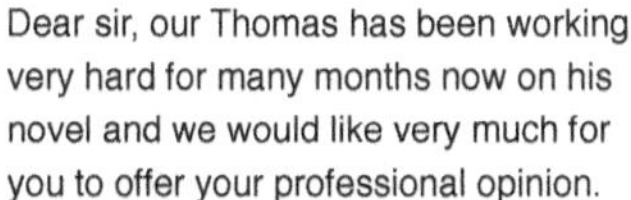

I almost deleted it before reading. A Facebook message that begins “Dear Sir” is not a typical way of attracting my attention and engaging my services, but the strange innocence of the message caught my eye before my finger tapped the delete key. Its fussy tone—“our Thomas”, “very much”, “professional opinion”—was so out of place in my Messenger App’s inbox. It had the air of a missive that had tumbled out of time from some long distant past, shed its yellow OHMS envelope, and somehow acquired a URL at the end.

Despite myself, I followed the link.

It was a standard free site: no custom domain and partially overlaid by scummy clickbait advertising that told me

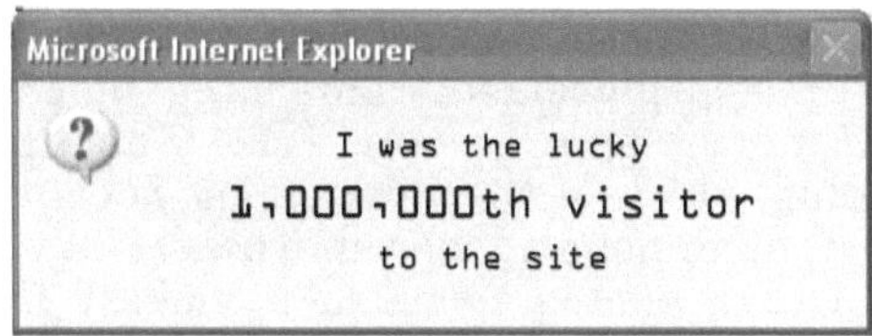

(wishful thinking) and assuring me that

I would be shocked

by the secret age-defying trick

discovered by some mum in Enoggera (nice touch) that the medical professions

don't want me to know about.

The site's title banner read *Thomas Bell: Writer* with his name arranged in the manner of a 1980s blockbuster novel—small given name perched atop a giant surname. Several long blog posts followed that I only skimmed, picking up phrases like "corporate dross" and "artistic integrity", and names like "Hemingway" and "Dickens".

Rather than read on, I returned to Facebook and to the "friend" who had sent me the message.

There was little of interest in Anita Bell's posts (mostly minion-themed platitudes), but her photos revealed little more than the online output familiar to millions of ordinary Australians (I mean the term in its non-political guise, hence the lowercase "o"): everyday, hard-working people suddenly putting on airs, pouting for the camera, straining themselves to reveal every last scrap of bulging tattooed, fake-tanned skin that will pass muster with puritan social network policies, the giveaway arm placement confirming that no one was behind the lens. I peered closely at the faces, wondering which of these might be *Thomas Bell: Writer*, though none appeared to be *writerly* in any sense. Other photos revealed a modest family's complement of birthdays, new cars, visits to South Bank. And, curiously, between the puffed up bulges and the happy snaps, Mrs. Bell had included a handful of starkly contrasting images: restrained and beautiful, mostly abstracted architectural, bright, flat and utterly devoid of people, early Jeffrey Smart paintings translated to the real world.

When I returned to Mrs. Bell's message to reply with polite refusal, I saw she had already sent more information.

> He writes on something called What-pad. He tells me has so many readers there he is overwhelmed with positive comments. But we dearly need for his work to take the next step to print so we are looking for a publisher for the novel. Despite all his hard work and research and teaching, he has very few contacts in the industry and we were hoping you might have some advise for him.

> Hello Anita, I don't usually do manuscript assessments.

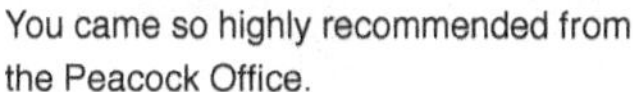

Oh great. The office dobbed me in for this? I took a deep breath and slowly typed my response.

> I really only have enough time to take a brief look and provide some generalised advice.

Before I could forward details of time and cost, Mrs. Bell had already replied.

Thank you so much Mr Falx! I am so pleased you are able to look at Tom's work. I would get him to reply directly to you, but he is out at the moment. He teaches a creative writing class at the local library. We are so proud of him.

The next message was a set of contact details and a link.

Is this the manuscript?

Yes

I opened the page in a separate browser tab. The page contained what looked like a synopsis of *The Mad Season: Book 1 of the Classic Works Cycle*, forty-one chapters by ThomasBell1877. From the stats, I could see the novel's readership was far from thriving as I had been promised: 61 reads and three "votes". Bell's avatar looked like a serious young writer, a face recognisably related to those from Mrs. Bell's images. The synopsis ominously took a liberal approach to capitalisation and punctuation.

Can you tell me what the novel is about?

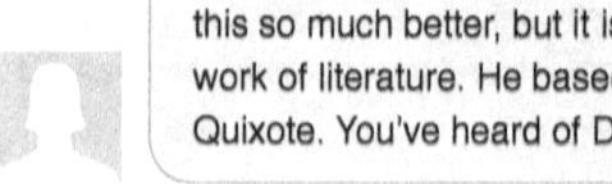

That would be wonderful. Thomas could explain this so much better, but it is intended as a classic work of literature. He based it on the novel Don Quixote. You've heard of Don Quixote?

I choked on a laugh, thankful that we weren't having this conversation face to face.

Yes. I'm pretty familiar with it.

You know how this plays out. One look at the synopsis was enough. The first few paragraphs contained PORTENTOUS ALL CAPS and in what followed I could already see dialogue that veered wildly between cliché, nonsense, and passages that looked suspiciously like cuts-and-pastes directly from Cervantes. I should have shut down the conversation there, but what drew me in deeper was the thought that this was the author's *mother* I was messaging and the sense of anxious optimism she radiated, even in plain text. I hoped I could find a graceful exit.

I guess Tom has spent some time over this.

Day and night. He quit his job last year so he could devote himself fully to his art. He was always a great reader, so different from his brothers and sisters, always borrowing books from the library, attending the free classes at the tafe. He teaches now when hes able and sometimes writes short opinion pieces online, but his heart is set on being a great novelist and seeing his name in print. What do you think of his work?

It's ambitious.

I should get Polly here to talk to you. She can tell you more about the novel.

That won't be necessary.

Shes quite an artist herself, takes really nice pictures. They have a beautiful daughter together. Ill go get her.

I noted with faint amusement the slow evaporation of Mrs. Bell's formal tone as a long pause in the conversation indicated she was away from the keyboard. While waiting, I returned to Mrs. Bell's images, taking a closer look at the beautiful architectural images. One was tagged *Polly Marston*, a link that led me to a profile of a serious young artist—dark eyes and no pouting—seemingly as comfortable in front of a camera as she was behind it. The handful of her public images suggested an eye for composition, a modest social life, and the suggestion of a baby at home.

Hello

Hi. Is this Polly?

Yes. I'm sorry Tom is out. Thank you so much for agreeing to read his work. After so much time on it, we all have such high hopes. It's been hard for us these last coup elf years and Tom really needs some success. We all do.

Great. Just great.

What do you want to know about the novel?

I didn't want to know anything about the novel.

This is a first draft?

Parts of it. It takes the story of Quixote and translates it to modern day New York with Quixote himself as a presidential candidate. Tom is always saying that all the classics need is an exciting new setting, some guns and explosions and sex to reach more people.

I can see parts of the original story in there. Is that deliberate?

Tom says he's allowed to do that because it's in the public domain. Is that true?

I made a few attempts at a response before settling on:

Not exactly.

There was a painful pause. I could picture the two women looking at each other, confirming silently between them that I did not appreciate Tom.

Tom has been very unwell these last few months. The novel is the one thing thats kept him going. Hes put everything into it. The novel belongs to all of us.

I took some extra work and Toms mum has been looking after the baby. Toms pumped about landing a big international publishing contract. I'm not so sure, but from the kind of books i see on the shelves at target, i reckon this is just as good.

No one would look at the manuscript in its present state and it would never likely become the classic he hoped for. Then again, plenty of badly written books had become raging bestsellers. Why shouldn't Thomas Bell's join them?

International markets don't often pick up works that have been first published in Australia, though.

That's what I thought.

I tell Tom that to publish it in Australia, he should set the novel here, not in America, but he's convinced that Australia is a stupid place to set a story. It's mean and stupid and has no romance about it and no one's interested in what happens here anyway. He can be a bit stubborn like that.

All writers can be precious with their work.

I'll read the manuscript and send a report to you. I won't be able to provide a detailed edit but I can certainly give him some feedback on improving the work and maybe some ideas towards options for publication. Thanks for getting in touch with me.

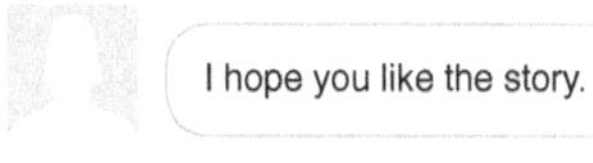

I hope so too.

Not a word of a lie.

Though I can't say I read the novel closely, I gave it more attention than I had initially intended. I slogged my way through its forty-one sometimes meandering, sometimes lurching, always curious chapters with the suspicion that I was the butt of an elaborate practical joke. What was most frustrating about the story was the moments Bell swept away the clichés, the obsession with classic texts, and the inexplicable character motivations (why *did* candidate Quixote pull a gun on campaign manager Sancho Panza in chapter fifteen?) and I glimpsed all too briefly an original and possibly even exciting voice floundering in all that detritus.

What could my appraisal say about *The Mad Season*? (Why was it even called that?) The novel was only, in journalistic phrase, "worth a paragraph", but of what nature should that paragraph be? My duty was very plain and the descriptions that immediately sprang to mind—"bewildering", "uneven", "libellous", even "execrable"—were ones I would steel myself to use had Thomas Bell himself made the initial approach for an appraisal. Had Bell subjected me to the kind of grandiose self-conceit I drew from his blog and from the ways in which his mother and girlfriend spoke of his work, I would have happily savaged the novel, consigning it forever to a forgotten corner of a crowded world wide web with nothing but a few reads and a handful of "votes".

But the message was destined not for the author's inbox, but his mother's. I thought mostly of her and Polly, people who probably should have known better, but continued to believe in the mastery of his work despite all available evidence. They were proud of his modest achievements and willed him on. In *some* ways, he was incredibly fortunate to have such supportive people around him.

And, clearly, I was a sucker.

So, what did I say?

"Thank you, Thomas, for the opportunity to read your novel, *The Mad Season*. Though the work will require some extensive editing before it will be ready to present to a prospective publisher, I can see much to admire in the way you handle the action sequences—*blah blah blah*—the research you have clearly put in resonates well but perhaps a more subtle way to introduce—*yaddah yaddah yaddah*—with some work I can see the piece finding a place with a publisher of contemporary thrillers or—*etc etc etc*."

I forwarded the report—appropriately, containing germs of truth buried under mountains of waffle—and invoiced Mrs. Bell for a fraction of my usual rate.

The next day, I was startled to find a tall, pale young man waiting for me at the office. He sported a thin red beard and shabby clothes and anxiously jiggled his leg. His face was drawn with dark, almost bluish lips, and one hand remained clutching his belly as though he had nausea. He smelled of cigarettes.

"Mr. Falx?"

"Yes?"

"Thomas Bell."

He handed me a business card that replicated the bestseller wordmark from his blog (#branding).

"Thanks for your feedback."

"Um, no worries." I fumbled for my keys to open the door.

"I was just wondering why you didn't mention Quixote's evolution over the course of the story."

"Well—"

"Because it seemed to me that that's the heart of the story and it was just a bit disappointing that you didn't mention it at all."

"See, with an appraisal like that—"

"It doesn't matter, anyway. Every reader emphasises something different in the story; I know that. Really, I wanted to thank you for taking the time to read it and provide such detailed feedback. I've taken some of your advice—I've been working on it all night—and I was wondering if you could take it to some publishers for me."

I allowed myself a chuckle. "Tom, I'm not an agent."

"But you are in the industry. You know people. You will help me in a way no one else can. This novel is my one shot, the one chance I have to reach the big time. You've read it. You know this. Look, I've done so many different courses over the years and I've read so many books—I know books aren't appreciated in this country—but to have had the time and attention of someone of such taste—"

I'll never know where that sentence might have gone; it was consumed by a violent coughing fit. I opened the door to office and half-stepped through, making it clear that I was not inviting Tom inside. When the author straightened himself and looked back at me, I could see his eyes were bloodshot.

"Tom, I will help you in whatever way I can, but—"

But? Go on. But *what*, Falx?

"—but you shouldn't put too much emphasis on one manuscript. Stories succeed and fail all the time due to factors beyond anyone's control, least of all the author's. And this story—"

His shoulders slumped and I could feel my willpower fading. *Sucker!*

"—well, it may not appeal to everyone."

"It's a classic! It's a classic retold for today's audience! But you must be busy. Can we maybe meet later to talk about this some more?" he puffed his chest out as far as it would allow, but failed to mask the anxiety in his voice.

"Well, I don't—"

"Oh, I'm sorry. Am I overstepping my boundaries?"

"No, it's okay. Sorry, no. How about after work this evening?"

One drink, I promised myself. I spent the day steeling myself to cast Bell off with the simple message to find another outlet for his creativity. We arranged to meet at a local bar close to my office. When I arrived I found him flanked by two women, clearly Mrs. Bell and Polly (one hand rocking a pram back and forth). Though they both spent most of their time staring at their phones—Mrs. Bell on Facebook and Polly with her free hand on what looked like a photo editing app—their support and infectious sense of excitement at what they thought was transpiring gave the author a second wind. His chest was fuller, his face redder, though his hacking cough remained.

"This is his big chance," said Mrs. Bell.

"Who would have thought?" said Polly. "It's only a matter of time before we land a big publisher in Sydney or Melbourne."

Over a few beers (yes, more than one), pausing only to step outside for a smoke, Tom talked Art and raved about his mission and the genius that was in him that MUST. COME. O

He banged his fist on the table repeatedly though, I must admit, weakly. His girlfriend and mother nodded their agreement, even the baby gurgled her support. When Polly looked up from her screen and regarded her partner, tears filled her eyes.

We've all met Thomas Bell, the unhappy soul

whose talent extends only as far as admiring others and yet who is cursed with a desire to create. And share. What drives them to continue? Revering the successful few, even those who fall short of genius, is easy. They may (and do) suffer for their art, but their efforts delight the world and they are rewarded with recognition, fame, money, whatever. But what of the multitude of Thomas Bells, who endure all the suffering, but never reach the prize?

The Mad Season did not land a big publisher in Sydney or Melbourne. It didn't land a small publisher in Brisbane or Adelaide or Perth or Hobart or Darwin, even after Bell retitled it (at my suggestion) *Primary Motive*. It may surprise you to know that I actually tried. It surprised me. I slipped it into the inboxes of a few people I knew, surrounded by caveats and suggested changes. I mentioned his name at a few launch events to agents, booksellers, and editors. I embarrassed myself for him, for Polly and Mrs. Bell. But it was clear enough still what I had deduced the moment I first laid eyes on the text. Thomas Bell would never be a successful author. He wouldn't see his name arranged in that blockbuster format unless he himself did so. Thomas Bell wasn't a writer. He was a reader. He knew stories and he could even copy some aspects of storytelling well. But he wasn't a writer.

I know what you're thinking. You're thinking it was cruel of me to lead Tom on like that. I should have sucked it up, pulled the man aside and told him to find another profession. People with a passion for stories can find themselves in the most extraordinary careers. I know this better than anyone. And you're right, of course. I should have done that. But every time I plucked up the nerve to deliver him my honest assessment of his prospects, he would reintroduce me to his two-person support crew/cheer squad and their enthusiasm would spur me on to try *just one more time.*

I'm thankful I didn't charge him anything after that initial assessment. After all, I did the man no service.

Time passed. I made occasional but regular attempts to find a home for Tom's novel to no avail and his breathing became ever more laboured, his cough worsened.

Ugh. Need I continue?

Thomas Bell died early last week. The lung cancer metastasised to his brain and progressed quickly from there. He was in considerable pain in his last months, but his mother and girlfriend stayed beside him to the end. His novel remained on Wattpad and gained a handful of new readers in that time, but no more "votes".

I joined Polly, Mrs. Bell, and the rest of his family at his funeral.

"He made his mark," said Polly through her tears as we left the crematorium, "and I will make sure that *one day* the world will know the name Thomas Bell." She turned to me: "Tell me, Mr. Falx, what do you know about ebooks?"

HI, I'D LIKE TO ADD YOU TO MY PROFESSIONAL NETWORK ON LINKEDIN.

I WAS eager to continue working, despite the late hour. I was confident that, ensconced in my study and illuminated only by the glow of my screen, I wouldn't disturb my sleeping family upstairs. Working late meant a welcome long stretch of uninterrupted concentration, so long as I'd had enough coffee to stay awake. Only once have I fallen asleep at the desk, accidentally filling 153 pages of "r"s as I dribbled over the spacebar. That wouldn't happen tonight. I was pleased with how this was going, this strange business of remixing someone else's work, acknowledging it, modifying it, spinning off from it to create something new. It was liberating.

I picked at the text on my screen: reading, highlighting, deleting and writing, my fingers hitting the keys in manic bursts, harder than necessary. I was some way into a new story when the first email notification slid into view.

"Hi, I'd Like to Add You to My Professional Network on LinkedIn…"

Ugh. I hovered the mouse over the trash button, when noticed the name of the "sender". I paused for a moment.

Martin Finn.

I wrote a story years ago about a character with exactly that name. I flipped to my mail client and looked more closely at the profile picture in the message. An out-of-focus image of a generic middle-aged man. If I squinted at the photo, the man appeared not dissimilar to how I imagined Martin Finn would have looked (in as much as I'd thought about him at all in the years since writing the story).

Had this Martin Finn read my story and wanted to get in contact? More likely, I reasoned with myself, it was a coincidence. There must be hundreds, thousands, of Martin Finns in the world and plenty of randoms would like to add me to their Professional Networks. Meh. I shrugged internally. What the hell. I followed the link to accept Martin's invitation.

404 PAGE NOT FOUND

We couldn't find that page. It either moved or doesn't exist anymore.

Huh. I blinked at the screen. Curious. A text message arrived at my phone, cutting through the silence. Years ago I set my text message ringtone to the sound of a solemn American announcer saying, "*Sycamore is open*," a sample extracted from a great sound collage (google the phrase if you really need to know its source). But that night, the sound of a voice emerging from my pocket made me jump. I took a deep breath and pulled out the phone. The message came from a number I didn't recognise.

Today 12:37 AM

Fifteen years.

My skin prickled and an uneasy fog filled my chest.

Who is this?

Delivered

You decide, in some demented part of your brain, to condemn me to locked-in syndrome. You give me a brain haemorrhage. You take away my ability to move, to speak. And you consign me to a nursing home—now the damaged male hero Australian writers so love—all so you can make your bland observations about communication and creativity.

I stared at the message, my hands shook slightly. This was some trick, some elaborate stunt being pulled on me by—

—by who? The story I wrote about Martin had been published years earlier. Who even remembered it now but me?

And then you left. For fifteen years we have had to live with the wreckage you made of me. I have survived this far—longer than anyone expected—and my children are now grown up knowing only a father who needs constant care. Why did you do this to us?

My thumbs paused as I scrambled to think of something to say.

It was just a story.

Delivered

Pshaw!

I squinted at the word, wondering if it was a typo. Wait. If this was Martin Finn—*my* Martin Finn—then something didn't make sense.

How are you sending these messages?

Delivered

Assistive technology has moved on from pointing to letters on a communication board. But you left all that behind, didn't you?

I began several replies to this, but deleted all of them. If this was a trick, it was someone who not only knew the character and my writing, but knew me, my history, knew how I work, how I think about my characters. The kind of stuff that never makes it to the page.

Another email arrived.

"Hi, I'd Like to Add You to My Professional Network on LinkedIn..."

I had only enough time to register the name on the email—Mavis Jolley—before Skype pinged awake with an incoming call.

Mavis Jolley. What the hell was going on?

I answered the call. What else could I do? At the other end of the connection a poorly positioned image of old lady stared levelly somewhere off camera, her left ear cut off at the side of the frame.

"It *is* you," she said.

Even through the pixellation and connectivity fuzz I could see how worn down and wretched she had become. Her long white hair was tied back into a loose bun, her shoulders slumped, her skin was grey, and what I could see of her downcast eyes filled me with regret.

"Hello Mavis," I said weakly. "How..." I cleared my throat, "...how are you?"

"What was the point?"

"I'm sorry?"

"What was the point? My daughter was afflicted, my husband was hounded to his death, and I was left alone for years. And what did you do? You dangled an apparition of my daughter before me while floodwaters rose, you tormented me with her before you drowned me in the service of your ham-fisted attempt at magical realism." She squeezed her eyes shut and turned away for a moment. She might have muttered something under her breath, but I couldn't be certain. "What was the point," she finally repeated, "of making my life such a misery?"

It was true. I had indeed done all these things to Mavis. And here she was: a broken person at the other end of a Skype call handing me a one-star review of the story that featured her.

"The magical realism thing made a nicer ending than I originally planned. You were supposed to—" I was interrupted by another call request. Mavis, without acknowledging me, accepted the new caller into our conversation. The new connection was poor, even worse than the one with Mavis, but the face of the caller was unmistakable. Her hair was bright pink and, as she spoke, her arms waved around maniacally leaving a pixellated trail in front of her face.

"You're a piece of work," Leith spat, dispensing with a traditional greeting. "You set me up to make a bloody fool of myself. I was vulnerable after that car accident and you send in Brad the physio to toy with my emotions. Jesus! *Brad*? You set me up as the tough young heroine who should never be defined by her relationship to any man, let alone *Brad*. I deserved better than that and you know it. You always worried that it wasn't plausible I would fall for a jerk like that and it wasn't, but—*hell*—you went and made me do it anyway."

Before I could defend myself, another caller. This one purported to be from a ".ru" domain and although the name was rendered in Cyrillic script, I recognised it instantly (thank you, otherwise useless university courses in Russian):

Николай Чеков.

"Hello Kolya," I said (I never thought of him by his full name, Nikolai).

"You killed my father," he said, "and left me to be raised by a paranoid mother so that I could be the innocent child in the *bildungsroman* you were so insistent on creating."

"You got the girl," I said. "Nice to see you too," I added, tartly I must admit.

"One kiss before—at your direction—her brothers chased me down and tried to beat me."

"Oh yeah. I forgot about that."

The three of them glowered at me.

"Listen," I said, putting to one side (with some effort) the enormous question of how this could be happening, "I get it. You're all angry and you blame me for having created the situations you find yourselves in. I understand, really I do. You've made your point. But what now? What is it you want from me?"

"First we want an answer," said Kolya.

"Why?" said Leith. "Why did you have treat us like something you leave out on the footpath?"

Yes.

The single word arrived by text to my phone from Martin, who was apparently following our conversation somehow. Whether intended or not, it echoed the only "lines" (yes and no) I gave him in the story I wrote about him. I remembered that I had made Martin a writer too, prior to his stroke. Surely he was well aware of what was needed to create a story and the recurring tropes of our profession. I even recreated extracts from his work at one point. I knew his heroes were just as damaged as mine.

Rather than look at their images on my screen, I looked directly into the camera so as to eyeball everyone more effectively. "It was necessary," I said.

"Treating us terribly," said Mavis, "was *necessary*?"

"If you all led perfectly comfortable lives in which nothing bad happened, then there would be no story to tell. Without some kind of hardship, there's no story and without a story none of you would exist at all."

They considered this.

"So we exist to suffer?" said Kolya.

"Well you came out better than anyone else here. You got away from the brothers without a beating."

"But why leave me so lonely for all those years?" said Mavis.

"Whose choice was that? What happened after your husband died was never part of the story. Anything could have happened in that time. You could have taken a lover, maybe. Someone younger? I don't know."

"You know that's not in my nature."

"Yes, okay, fair enough. But it was a short story. Whatever happened outside the story wasn't relevant. You could have made your own life in the years I had no interest in."

"But I was always going to end up in the same place, wasn't I?"

"There was no need for my paralysis to be permanent," said Leith. "That was just plain spiteful on your part."

"But without that permanence, you would never have let your guard down enough around Brad and no one would have seen through your bravado. Then there's no story." I sighed. "I have written plenty of stories that have gone nowhere, tied themselves up in knots, or whatever. I've changed stories halfway through. Some characters I haven't just killed off; I've deleted them. Others have never seen the light of day. What's worse? At least you endure. You're on fixed pages in ink and paper, not sitting in a document nested within a series of subfolders in my Dropbox."

I stunned them into a brief silence before I continued.

"What else?"

"Huh?" said Leith.

"You wanted an answer. That was my answer. What else do you want?"

"You know what we want," said Mavis. "We want you to re-write us."

"What?"

"Change the story," said Kolya. "It is in your power to make us happy. Give me dignity."

"Give me my daughter," said Mavis.

"Give me my legs!" cried Leith.

Yes.

I held a hand to my forehead and counted to ten in my head preparing to respond when yet another call joined our party line. Who the hell was Thomas Bell?

"Hello?" I said, peering at the pathetic figure crouched in a darkened room.

"What kind of monster are you?" said Bell, apparently unaware he was late to the meeting. "You give me a dream I can't possibly achieve, then, as if that's not enough, you kill me off! You gave me brain cancer, you bastard! Brain cancer! What did I ever do to you? I just wanted to see my name in print."

Print?

Oh. It was *that* Thomas Bell.

"Okay, hold it!" I said, throwing my hands up at him. "You're not even my character. That was a remixed story based on another source. If you want someone to blame for your miserable life, blame Marcus Clarke."

A harsh static noise emerged from the computer's speakers. I tried to turn the volume down, but it didn't work.

"We're blaming you," said Leith.

"Make us whole again," said Mavis. "Re-write our stories."

"Or what? You'll keep annoying me with LinkedIn requests?"

"We can do much more than that," said Kolya.

The static from the speakers grew in intensity, filling my study with white noise.

"We are already inside your machine and on your network," said Bell. "We're on the electronic files you've left strewn across all your devices. We're inside the documents you have slaved over for twenty years, right back to the beginning of what you laughably call a career. You may have ensured that I cannot write, but it doesn't take much skill to erase."

"Erase?"

"All your work," said Leith. "Everything you've written, even the backups. We're everywhere and we can wipe it all out. You reckon you can delete characters, well we can delete a part of you too. We can erase everything. If you still have the stomach for this, you'll have to start again from the beginning."

The expression on each of their faces didn't change noticeably, but I felt their determination through the pixels. Where before they pleaded, now they demanded. The noise had become deafening and a part of me wondered why it hadn't woken anyone else in the house. I shook my head and held a hand to my ear. The noise wasn't coming from the speakers. It was in me.

"But if you erase the work," I said through the din, "you'll erase yourselves too."

"We endure," Kolya smiled. "You said so yourself. We are published in paper and ink. The rest of your work, though, and the years of your life you have devoted to it; it will all be gone."

"You're bluffing," I said, possibly for the first time in my life. When does anyone get to say that outside a story? "You're full of sh—" My voice caught on the last word, but I think I got the message across.

"Care to risk it?" said Bell.

I shook my head, not in disagreement, but more instinctively, as though I could dislodge the noise from my ears. I leaned back from the screen. Green modem lights blinked from the darkness of the far corner, indicating the movement of data between my computer and the network. I told myself this was ridiculous, my characters couldn't exist and they couldn't delete my files. But rationalisation couldn't stop my heart thumping and sweat falling in drips down my face. My characters had contacted me via LinkedIn, text messages and Skype. Maybe whatever technique they had invented for deleting my files would also rely on an internet connection. Maybe. The modem was a good two metres from my desk. If I made a move to unplug it, I would have to be fast.

...five, four, three...

"Re-write our stories," said Leith.

...two, one...

"Never!"

...zero.

As I leapt from the desk, the noise in my ears abruptly vanished and the screen blinked off. Plunged into darkness, I tripped over a guitar stand, knocking the instrument to the floor, and sending a discordant thump resonating through the floorboards and bouncing off the walls. I scrambled over the floor towards the still blinking green light, grabbed the box and pulled it with some force out from wall. The power point threw a brief blue spark and the modem died in my hands.

I stood in a silence broken only by mild tinnitus and the cry of a bush stone-curlew from somewhere outside.

It was a lull that didn't last long.

Three sharp knocks—it's always three—at the front door skewered me again with fear and a message pinged my phone, which was, of course, still on and connected.

"Hi, I'd Like to Add You to My Professional Network on LinkedIn…"

I turned a light on, relieved we still had power, and approached the front door.

"Who is it?" I said through the frosted glass to the silhouette on the other side in a voice that came from someone else, someone very far away from me.

When no response was forthcoming, I realised I had probably whispered the question.

"Who is it?" I said again, this time stronger, bolder. Good. Nice work.

"Marcus Andrew Hislop Clarke."

I stared at the outline of the figure. "Who are you really?" I said in more of a squeak.

"I am the unwilling collaborator on a peculiar work you apparently have seen fit to create. I implore you, sir, open the door!" When I made no move, he added, "I give you my word I will not try to harm you."

"What do you want?"

"I wish merely to see the face of the man who has butchered my prose."

Despite myself, despite my fear, and despite all good sense, I opened the door.

"Hello, Mr. Clarke," I said after clearing my throat.

He shook my hand and bowed his head. Unconsciously, I returned the gesture and allowed him inside. He appeared younger than me and quite a bit shorter. His hair was parted in the middle and his beard was trimmed neatly. His clothes were rough, but not too obviously historical (he wore trousers rather than breeches, a wide sensible necktie rather than a garish cravat or bow, and no hat). His good manners barely disguised an irritable and prickly demeanour. He sniffed at my writing space and remarked that it looked more like a music room. His accent surprised me. Having immersed myself in the very Australian-ness of his stories, I had readily overlooked the fact he was English. He enquired blandly about my framed posters: a souvenir from the *24-Hour Book* project and a quote from McCarthy's *The Road*. His movements were stiff and he regarded everything, including me, with piercing intensity: evaluating, judging.

"Can I…can I get you something?"

He accepted my offer of a drink after first establishing (with some surprise) that we had no tea in the house. I poured us each a glass of Tasmanian whisky I had been saving for a special occasion and we adjourned to the living room. Clarke was clearly intrigued by its arrangement—two couches around a large black rectangle—but didn't ask me about it.

"You seem distracted," he said.

"My characters," I stammered. "I'm not sure if I got to the modem in time, if I saved my work."

"There will be more work and there will be more characters to fill it."

"Did you have anything to do with them… finding me…?"

He looked mildly bemused. "Sir, your characters are your own affair. If they seek you out, it is through their own means."

"I knew I treated them badly—I mean, we kind of have to, don't we—but I never realised just how low I'd taken some of them. I'd forgotten how many I'd killed off or abandoned or whatever."

"It's of no matter," Clarke waved a dismissive hand. "Characters are dispensable. They may attempt to seize the writer's pen, but their efforts must always be demonstrated as illusory. You must know this."

"You *showed* it."

He voiced a satisfied grunt.

"Do you really think what I'm doing with your work is butchery?" I said. "From your stories and from what I've read about you, you seemed adventurous. I thought you would welcome this kind of experiment."

He took slug from the glass and, with an appreciative nod, swirled the remaining liquid around the ice. Eventually, rather than answer my question, he asked his own.

"What is it you wish to achieve?" he said.

I hate it when people do that. I thought for a moment and said, "I want to create a book that seems to have fallen through time. I've held a copy of *Holiday Peak* as you'd originally published it and other similar books that were published after your—" I baulked at the word "death".

"I never imagined those volumes would survive to see such a distant future."

"I could tell. They're fragile objects now, but we look after them. Your work lives on, but it is now most easily accessible via machines. The same machines we use to write. We have tools now that allow us to write in new ways and it's easier than ever to take existing texts and break them into pieces, modify them, turn them into something different. It's a different kind of creative act from penning something from scratch, but it *is* a creative act." Trust me, after years of doing what I do, statements like that just roll out of me. Before he could respond, I continued: "And like any adaptation, to do it well, you have to respect the source."

"Respect?"

"Do you know what Mark Twain said about you?"

He frowned and shook his head.

"It was after you...well...it doesn't matter. Look, I've got it here somewhere." He watched me closely as I excused myself to shuffle through the documents at my desk. When I returned, he listened with interest as I read aloud.

"'I not only regret, but feel surprised that

the Selected Works of Australia's only literary genius—a genius such as you will not see again for many a long year—should be out of print. Through the courtesy of his widow I obtained a copy of the work after failing to buy one anywhere. And such a work, such reading, such power. It was just the sort of reading to banish from one's thoughts such pain as I have been suffering. The subjects so interesting, and their treatment so brilliant and fascinating. No works of such a man should be left unpublished. It is the duty of Australians to assist the widow of so great a writer in publishing his works. I may tell you that we think a deal more of Marcus Clarke in our country than I am sorry to think you do here.'

"He said that in 1895," I continued, "and it's still relevant today. Our cultural cringe had set in before we'd even federated as a nation."

I had no idea if he understood any of what I said, but he seemed to take it in his stride.

"Are people then no longer familiar with my work?" he said.

"Well, a lot of people are still familiar with *His Natural Life*, or at least know it was a big budget mini-series in the 80s. A lot of people over a certain age would have seen it and remember."

"Mini-series," he said the words not as a question, but more as an experiment in adopting my language.

"Yeah, except they called it *For the Term of His Natural Life*, which I must admit has a better ring to it. It was a big deal: Colin Friels and Diane Cilento and that. It wasn't the first adaptation. There was a silent film in 1927 and a stage-play too. A couple of years ago, there was even an interactive app for the iPad based on it. It was pretty good from what I remember. I downloaded it at the time, but I deleted it when I ran out of space."

He took some time to process what I was saying before responding.

"If you wish," he said, "as I deduce from your rhetoric, that my stories be more widely read, then why make these changes to them? Can they not stand on their own?"

"Of course they can. They do. I've taken a lot of care to ensure that where I present your text, it matches the original works line by line. The only exceptions I made were to clean up obvious typos and to remove that casually racist one-liner from 'Hunted Down'. Oh, and the passing reference that Mordecai was Jewish, which was there for no apparent reason." Clarke set his glass down without taking his narrowed eyes off me. "So yes, I changed a few things that had no real impact on the story and, to be honest, I didn't want in there. It's been 144 years since you published that story and we still have to put up with way too much of that sh—" I choked on the word, cleared my throat. "I only mention it now because I suspect those asides reflected more the times in which you wrote, rather than any deeply held personal beliefs. Am I right?"

He considered this in silence, shifting his gaze from me to the flat black rectangle in our living room. The years between us had reduced to barely a couple of metres and the vast gulf between our respective ages seemed smaller than ever. His expression gave me no hint of his thoughts, but I wanted to think I might have touched a nerve, shared the sadness and mourning for a nation that has lost its innocence, but learned too little in the process. This is what had been gnawing at me long before my characters had set upon me, before the poor writer, before besmirching Bullocktown's circus, before I set about remixing anything and merely read. What did Clarke observe about who we were and what does it say about who we've become? We shrink in meek obedience in the face of authority, even as we pull faces behind its back. We're bold only with a bellyful to beat to submission anyone on a lower rung. We are relaxed and friendly (we lie to ourselves), but only for the right kind of visitor. And at the same time, we refuse to acknowledge the festering wounds of our own dispossession. We glorify the ordinary as though it's an end in and of itself. We aspire to be aspirational, not once pausing to wonder why the elites loudly denounce "elites" in our ears while they make craters in the very bush Clarke celebrated and burn its earth for a few more dollars. We pave over anything undesirable and build a complex on its plot; the property values are too good to waste. We goad the gullible to hate, then throw our hands up in despair when the inevitable blood returns to us. Always someone else can carry the blame. The rats of the culture wars wrestle in filth for the right to some kind of Australian soul. And in the mirror we see only the worst of ourselves.

I wanted to say these things, but I didn't. Of course I didn't. There may be people who can articulate such ideas concisely without the benefit of multiple drafts, but I'm not one of them. And so I sat with Marcus Clarke in silence, choking on volumes of regret and disappointment. He took note of my impotent turmoil and poured us each another glass of whisky, emptying the bottle. No ice. His expression had softened somewhat and I hoped that he sympathised with me.

"At least," he said, holding up his glass to me, "the book endures."

But my questions remained hanging in the air between us and still the elder author—the *genius* proclaimed by Twain himself—maddeningly refused to answer.

"I must know," I said as we clinked glasses,

"was I right to make those changes? Was I right to do what I've done with your work and your books? Is it something you yourself would have done had you been publishing in the early twenty-first century and not the late nineteenth?"

He laughed at this. "I cannot tell you that, sir."

"Why?" I said. "I know it's hypothetical, but you're here now and what better opportunity to ask the question?"

"I cannot tell you what I think. I can only reflect back to you what you already know about me."

"What do you mean?"

"I could respond definitively to your query, sir, but that would take this story even further into the realm of fantasy. The depiction of me here is based on reality and mild conjecture. As a result, I am a sketch at best, based on the rather scanty research I know has gone into this volume. I cannot provide you with any insights into my character that you do not already have at your disposal. You have my biography. You have my work. That is all."

"You're telling me this is a story?"

"It is indeed, sir."

I looked around the room, confirming this was my actual living room. I pinched myself for good measure. "Doesn't feel much like a story to me."

"I assure you, sir. I'm no more a real author than you are," he said blithely before taking a sip of his drink.

"Thanks," I laughed, "for the vote of confidence, Mr. Clarke."

He frowned, apparently missing my point. "Think to yourself what is more likely: that Marcus Clarke has returned to discuss your work with you or that this is an artifice, designed for purposes beyond our knowledge? This," he held a hand to his chest, "doesn't represent *me*. It doesn't capture who I am. Or who I *was*. You and I exist only to advance a story."

"Oh come on. This is bullish—" again I choked. "What the hell, why can't I get the word out?"

"The author—the real author—has decided you cannot." Clarke loosened his tie and leaned back on the couch, looking reasonably satisfied with himself. "Perhaps it's a stylistic choice."

I didn't believe him, not completely, but his logic was hard to fault. I was sharing a drink with someone who had been dead for 135 years, who had turned up at our door unannounced after my characters had attempted to erase my career and sent me flailing about the study, all of which had somehow not woken my family upstairs. I realised, suddenly, how implausible all this sounded.

Wait.

I've told this story before. A character who discovers his existence is fictional. And that story doesn't end well for him. It never ends well for my characters. What does that mean for me?

"Maybe," I said, "we should try to find *him*."

"Find who?"

"The real author. The one who is writing these words and making the decisions for us."

"Sir," he chuckled. "That cannot happen. He may be sitting somewhere exactly like this room, but he is beyond our reach. You know as well as I do that every story contains layers. There are characters, and beyond them there's an author implied in the text, and, beyond the implied author, the actual author who wrote the words. Your characters found you, but all they really found was another character. This is not reality. Beyond us, there's always another reality, another writer. If we were to seek him out, all we would find is more artifice. The characters from our stories were doing exactly that. They were looking for the real Mr. Groth and the real Mr. Clarke, not you, and not I. The author can keep building layers around us until we're exhausted or mad or both. This is our lot: you and

I sharing this excellent drink in the early hours of the morning. Enjoy it. Without conflict there is no story. If this is our conflict, I will accept it gladly. The story is a fine one and without that story you and I do not exist."

The birds outside began their daily chorus and the first light of dawn through the windows filled the room with grey luminosity.

"So what now?" I said. "There's just you and me. How do we finish the story? Do we introduce more characters? Do we duke it out? Do you want to just watch something on TV? Or do we leave the story dangling over a precipice in some kind of liminal state?"

"No," said Clarke. "I know how it should end."

Customers Who Bought This Item Also Bought

Page 1 of 16

Long Odds
› Marcus Clarke
18
$9.89

Holiday Peak and Other Tales
› Marcus Clarke
11
$7.99

Four Stories High
› Marcus Clarke
3
$9.88

His Natural Life
› Marcus Clarke
8
$10.54

People Also Search For

View 1+ more

Adam Lindsay Gordon

Henry Kendall

Norman Dawn

Henry Savery

Miles Franklin

Gabriel García Márquez

Anna Maria Bunn

Mark Twain

Most Helpful Customer Reviews

Ahead of time
By Balthazar Claës on January 11, 2016

Marcus Clarke was very funny and totally ahead of his time. Is this where the linkedin people got their idea for linkedin? Disappointed he didn't prdict YOLO or hashtags.

Don't waste your
By John Marston on January 14, 2016

Don't waste your money theres no hunting tips or even anything about hunting or guns. It was in this funny bag thing and bits fell out of it and the book has printing errors all the way through. Also there were ads. I use the bag to hold soap.

Trippy
By Tom Trowbridge on January 18, 2016

The bit where the text wobbles in and out is trippy. Thought it was me but it wasn't. Upside downy bit was cool too. Should read the rest some time.

Hunted Down and Other Tales first published 2016 by if:book Australia.

Third edition published 2018.

Dedication and 'Opinions of the Press' were first published in *The Peripatetic Philosopher*, by Marcus Clarke (writing pseudonymously as 'Q'), 1869, George Robertson.

'Hunted Down' was first published in *The Australasian*, 6 May 1871.

Cover design by George Saad with illustration 'The Poet' by Richard Dagley from Death's Doings, in *Twenty-Four Plates, Designed and Etched* by R. Dagley, 1827.

'The Poor Artist' was first published as part of the 'Noah's Ark' column in *The Australasian*, 13 July 1872. The primary source used for this volume comes from *Four Stories High*, 1877, A. H. Massina & Co.

'How The Circus Came To Bullocktown' was first published in *The Australasian*, 20 August 1870 and 3 September 1870. The primary source used for this volume comes from *Holiday Peak and Other Tales*, 1873, George Robertson.

'How The Circus Came To Bullocktown' uses code from *The Deletionist*, 2013, developed by Amaranth Borsuk, Jesper Juul and Nick Montfort. It is licensed under a GPL v2 license. http://thedeletionist.com/

✻ 'How The Circus Came To Bullocktown' contains quotations from John Timbs *Curiosities of London*, 1867, J. C. Hotten, pp 59-61.

+ 'How The Circus Came To Bullocktown' contains a quotation from Charles Hindley (ed.) *Tavern Anecdotes and Sayings: Including the Origin of Signs, and Reminiscences Connected with Taverns, Coffee-houses, Clubs, Etc*, 1875.

Special thanks to the National Library of Australia, State Library of Victoria, and State Library of Queensland, without whose efforts in preserving and making accessible Australian literary heritage, this work would be impossible.

This work has been supported with funding by the Australia Council for the Arts.

Written by Simon Groth.
Edited by Aimée Lindorff.
Designed by George Saad.

Thanks also to Mez Breeze, Christopher Currie, Zoë Sadokiersi, Ryan O'Neill, Des Groth and Lisa Dempster.

A catalogue record for this book is available from the National Library of Australia

ISBN: 978-0-6483746-0-2